To Andree

The Gene Thief

Fiona McDill

may you always see the funny side of life

Fiona mc

authorHOUSE®

AuthorHouse™ UK Ltd.
500 Avebury Boulevard
Central Milton Keynes, MK9 2BE
www.authorhouse.co.uk
Phone: 08001974150

First published by AuthorHouse 4/22/2009

ISBN: 978-1-4389-4852-2 (sc)

This book is printed on acid-free paper.

Chapter 1

It was an unusually clear night with a warm easterly breeze gently rocking the dingy that James sat in, he liked to fish especially at night, he preferred to be on his own, and it gave him time to think.

James lived in a coastal town. In the summer, it was a hive with tourists coming from all corners of the globe. Most of them were golfers, as there was a first class golf course near by and it was cheaper to stay in the village than stay in the town where the prices were extortionate. There was a few came for the fishing as the waters around this part were rich with all kinds of fish. There were divers that also chose this area to dive in as there were many wrecks lying on the seabed and the tidal currents were not to strong which made it ideal for diving. Some of the locals cashed in on this and you could hire fishing boats with an experienced crew to take you to the best places to fish. There was even a business set up two years ago to take people out on a days diving. In the winter things were considerably quieter it was almost like a ghost town, there were still tourists but not nearly as many. James liked the village in the summer time the best, as there was a lot more happening. The school had a drama club and every year they put a show on. This year James played a part in it. He did not normally go in for these things but he had a crush on the girl who had the leading role and joined the club to get the chance to speak to her. However, when he approached her he could not speak to her and turned away with a red face. He had given the part of a lobster. Which had no speaking part and he thought that the headmaster had only given him the part because there was no other part? This made him feel even more awkward and he considered leaving the club but his mother had persuaded him to stay at least until the end of the show.

James lived with his mother Andrea, his father Julian, older brother Jack his twin sisters Sarah and Emma in a large house close to the harbour. From his bedroom window, he could see across the bay. There was a large driveway up to the front of the house. Which had lights put in that brightly lit up the drive? He loved to hear the car wheels crunch on the gravel. The garden at the back was full of vegetables. There was a small orchard also all of which Mr Thom the gardener had tended to

Their parents had disappeared three months ago. They were coming home after attending a funeral of a close school friend whom had died after a long battle against cancer, when without trace vanished. The police tried every avenue, checked phone records, bank statements asked for witnesses, checked surveillance cameras even went on television but nothing they were no further forward.

James will remember the lead up to the day they left forever. He had had an argument with his father, it was not even a big argument, his father wanted James to study harder at school, and he told him if his grades didn't improve he was going to ban him from going out in his boat. James had said to his father that he was studying as hard as he could. It was the first time that he had answered him back, and for his troubles, he landed up in his room grounded for the weekend. James had noticed that his father was not the same with him as he was with his brother and sisters. This began to bother him. He always been singled out; he would speak to his mother when she brought his tea up to him. When she did bring his tea up to him, he asked her "why does dad treat me different".

She looked at him, she knew he would ask this question at some point but she did not want it to be now. He was still too young to hear the answer; after all, he was not even a teenager he should not have to know yet. "He hasn't been keeping to well recently. And do you remember that Sally Waters"

"Yes" he replied,

"That's the lady who came to stay for a holiday at Christmas. She was not feeling to well and you and dad had to take her to the hospital. I remember because

I thought that it must have been horrible to be in the hospital when Santa came to see you in your bed to make sure that you had been good and that you were sleeping.

"Yes that's right," she said, stroking his hair. "We have just received a phone call to let us know that she isn't with us, that she is an angel and your dad and I have to go to her funeral".

James knew what a funeral was. He thought to himself that it should be his fathers, not Sally's funeral. Sally had been so much nicer. His mum kissing the top of his head brought him back from his thoughts. He liked the way she did that, he turned round to her, flung his arms around her neck, and buried his face in her hair. He could smell her perfume she always smelt nice. He could feel her hand rub rubbing his back. Maybe his father did not show any love towards him but his mum did and for that, he felt the luckiest boy in the world.

The next day his parents had packed the car with the luggage they need. Their father got into the car and waited until Andrea had gone round the kids giving out hugs, kisses, and the instructions what to do in an emergency. The last thing she said was "we will only be a few days take good care of each other. I love you all"

In addition, with her hand waving franticly out the window until the car was out of sight.

Chapter 2

Jack was eighteen and had left school to work in the family business, which his was first started by his grandfather and his brother nearly fifty years ago; they opened a coffee shop [rather served coffee in the back room of his great grandparent's house]. They now were the owners of two coffee houses; they were looking to open a third one in the next town to celebrate there up and coming fifty years of business. Jack kept himself busy with trying to keep the new shop and the celebration on track praying that their parents would turn up with some excuse as to their disappearance.

Sarah and Emma were seven and had taken the news of their parents bad they had night terrors wakening the completely house and possibly next-door as well. They spent a lot of time together alone. They both had been getting counselling but both were still trapped inside their own little worlds Jack was to busy to spend much time with them but was always home to read a bedtime story to them just like his father had done. James spent more time with them. He would always talk to them and ask questions, questions that gone unanswered He made their breakfast and a snack for school and walked them to school. At school they kept themselves to themselves and did the work in class, avoided the stares the nudges and the whispers and like, Jack prayed for their parent's safe return soon.

James was different. He was not sure why, but he knew his parents were not coming back. Which made him sad? He wanted to grieve for them, to let all the pent up feelings be felt released, to help Sarah and Emma come to terms with their loss. However, whenever he voiced his opinion his brother would blow his lid and yell at him. He had even hit him, which was a side to him James had never seen before. So from that day he became very scared of him. That day will forever be in James's mind. Jack had used James like a punch bag and had left James battered and bruised. His body had ached, and the bruises covered his arms, legs and torso. He had covered his head with his hands to protect it. For the first time in his life, James had feared for his life.

Chapter 3

James sat all alone in the dingy, looking up at the stars twinkling in the cloudless midnight blue skies. He could not help his mind returning to Jacks strange behaviour. For as long as he could remember, his older brother had been a kind, soft hearted, easygoing person. Recently he had changed. Perhaps the strain of their parents mysterious disappearance had not helped, nor the break up with his teenage sweetheart. Jack had known Bethany ever since he started school. They to sit beside each other in the class It was not love at first sight, Jack tormented her, he would pull her hair, which Bethany's mum used to plait every morning and secure the ends with ribbons. Sometimes Jack would pull the ribbons out and run round the playground chased by a screaming Bethany, only giving up when the bell rang summoning the children back to their classes. Bethany soon learned to give as well as she got. She would pretend to need her shoelace tied, duck under the table and swiftly tie Jack's laces together then patiently wait until Jack tried to walk. He fell down in front of the whole class who all started to roar with laughter but more embarrassing to Jack was the fact that he could not tie his own laces and had to get the teacher to tie them for him. Once when he tried to grab at her pink ribbons, she saw it coming and quickly pulled them out before Jack reached them. Then in front of all his mates, she held them out in front of Jacks face and said in the loudest voice she could manage said he could have her ribbons and that he would really suit pink. Jacks face reddened and he walked away. Bethany sat next to a very quiet subdued Jack for the rest of the day. Bethany began to feel a bit guilty so the next day she went over to where Jack was hanging out with one of his mates and asked to speak to him in private. They walked away from the other boy and Bethany told him that they should stop annoying each other and be friends. Jack thought for a moment then said that would be fine. The shook hands as a peace pact. Then Bethany went into her school bag and brought out a homemade cookie that her mother had made and handed it to Jack, who took it and broke it in half and gave Bethany the other half. They both turned and walked away feeling a sense of achievement. Things between them got better as time past. They started to do things together and Bethany came round to the house more and more. Then when they went to high school, they started to date. They got on really well, and sometimes they would even take James with them when they went to the pictures. They grew up together. James liked her because she would tell Jack off when he gave him a row. James hoped that they would get married one day, and that way she would always be there to stick up for him.

He had seen Bethany several times since they broken up. She always spoke to him and always asked after Jack. He wanted to ask her why they had split up but did not in case she got upset. He was not sure what to do if a girl got upset and started to cry because boys do not cry, they just want to fight and be macho. He thought that girls were strange. Tonight he wished that Jack were still dating Bethany because he needed someone on his side that could tell Jack off. However, not all the excuses James could think of could hide the truth. His brother scared him.

Chapter 4

James looked into the horizon and could just make out the inky black of the sea from the midnight sky. He thought about his mum, she was always putting her children first and knew when one of them troubled, as James had been many a time. Jack and the twins had jet-black curly hair, hazel eyes, and their skin always had a healthy tan. James had ginger hair [which was the brunt of every kid in school's jokes] his eyes were blue [his mum used to say they were like the Indian Ocean] and his skin was milk white [again the jokes were on him,]. When he had just started school, he came home nearly every day distraught and in tears. His mum would comfort him tell him it didn't matter what others say, he was her prince charming and no-one is perfect, it is what's inside that matters. Soon he ignored the taunts and jibes it no longer hurt him the way it used to.

Looking out to the horizon, he wondered how far the Indian Ocean was.

Rummaging though his backpack he pulled out the sandwich, he made earlier. Hewas not very hungry but ate a few mouthfuls, the broke up the remainder and dropped it into the water to entice the fish; it appears the fish are not hungry either.

James saw less of his brother as he worked more and more away from home. Spending most of his time at the new coffee shop, which had opened as planned to celebrate the fiftieth years of business. He had hired help to see that Sarah, Emma and James got the care that they needed the twins got on really well with her as they all knew Mary, she had been an auxiliary at the primary school that Jack was in, and she came to know the family. Therefore, Jack approached her to see if she would help them out. Mary helped the twins and encouraged them to speak about their parents. Soon they began to cope better with the disappearance of their mum and dad; they too now believed that they were not coming back. One afternoon when they came home from school, they went to James's room. There was a soft tap on his door and he could hear them fidget on the other side of the door he shouted for them to come in but they stayed on the other side. James went to the door and opened it to find them standing with there heads bowed looking at the floor. He knew something was bothering them so he took hold of their hands and led them into his room. Once the door had closed shut, the two of them had started to cry. He put his arms around them and held them tight. He could feel their little bodies shudder with every heartbreaking sob. He held them tight and kissed the top of their head, (he could remember his mother used to do that to them all. Jack was taller than his mum was and she could not reach the top of his head. However, she would wait until he was sitting down then kiss his head. James could remember thinking he hoped he never grew too tall or too old for his mother to kiss the top of his head). He waited until they were ready to speak. However, James knew what was coming. Through their sobs, they told him that they too believed something terrible had happened to their parents, and were concerned about what was going to happen to them. James was glad that they spoke to him and not Jack, he feared they might get the same as he did. When they said that they also thought that their parents were not coming back, together, the three of them held a secret service for them, and planted a tree in the garden as a place they could retreat to, remember, and reflect on the good times.

Chapter 5

James started working in the coffee shop nearest his school. It was for a few hours after school, also on a Saturday. He helped in the kitchen and got a small wage. He kept this quiet as was not supposed to work. He enjoyed the atmosphere and often thought about his great grandfather and great uncle and how different things would have been in their day.

It was a quiet, early evening when a man wearing a long black leather coat and a leather hat, came in and sat in the corner. James had been clearing some tables and looked up when the bell above the door tinkled to announce the arrival of customers. He looked around, saw the man, and seemed to be very transfixed by this man. He could not quite understand why, perhaps because he thought he looked like a baddie from a western. However, this man seemed to bring a sense of calm to James. A sound from one of the waiters brought James back to his senses. James cleared the rest of the tables, but watched the man. The man smiled and asked if they had been busy. James just nodded, he felt he should know this person but had never seen him before. Once he had finished his coffee the man rose from the table looked straight at James, said, "I'll see you later James", and left the shop.

It took him a second or two to realize that this stranger had called him by his first name. He ran to the door to ask how he knew his name, but when he reached the street the man had vanished leaving James to wonder whom he was and how did he know his name. James asked the waiter if the man that had just left was a regular.

"No, never seen him before, I don't think he's a local his accent sounded foreign" was the waiters reply.

"He knew my name," James said.

The waiter knew by the sound of James's voice that he was a bit on edge because of his encounter with the stranger and told him that it might just be a coincidence. He made James a special coffee and brought a currant bun which James loved, they were home baked by the waiters wife, both of them had worked in the shop for fifteen years. He had known James from the day he was born, he recalls the time he saw James's father hours after he was born. He came back to the shop and was in a foul mood. He was convinced that this baby was not his; he was very different from Jack his first-born son, Jack was like them dark hair, hazel eyes. This baby was a red head with a shock of thick spiky ginger hair. No-one in his genes had ever had ginger hair, he had Italian background, as did his wife. Adamant that this baby was not his he paid to have DNA tests. He stopped himself from accusing his wife from having an affair instead; he waited for the results from the test.

When he went to the hospital to see his wife he never looked at the baby. His wife got very upset with him, she knew what he was thinking and tried to assure him that there was nobody else that he and he alone was the only one for her. When she was told about the DNA tests that had been ordered by her husband that was the final straw, she wanted a divorce she wasn't going to be humiliated by him. This baby was his, how could he be so horrid to a small helpless baby and to the woman whom had married and set up home. She had helped with the business and had devoted her life to him. When the results came back, they got them just before they were due to leave from the hospital. The doctor brought them into his office and read the results. Beyond no doubt this was his son but no one could explain the ginger hair and the skin tone, it was almost white. The doctor told them they should be proud of their baby, he was healthy, and a happy wee soul. He had hardly ever cried, even now he was smiling at them. His wife made him carry the baby to the car. Then Andrea hade made him stop at the shop to show every one in there their new baby. If he did not want a divorce, he would have to accept that as the results said, this was his son.

The waiter helped James with the last of the clearing up, locked up the shop and took James home. He went in to the house and could hear the music and the giggles from his sister's room upstairs. He went to find the housekeeper Mary, it was not hard, and he could smell the cooking. Mary was busy making supper "the girls have some friends for a sleepover. Is there anything you would like to eat?"

She asked him

"No, I'm fine. I think there's going to be a lot of girly squeals and giggles tonight" he replied "I think so, hope you don't mind" Mary inquired.

"Not in the least. I am pleased that they are having fun. They have taken the disappearance of our parents really bad but I think they are moving on and dealing with it better" James replied with a smile.

Chapter 6

James stared out of his bedroom window he could see the sea which was calm, he could hear the giggles and squeals from the girls room along the hall and thought he needed to be alone not because of the noise, he was genuinely happy for the twins. However, he had the urge to be alone. He took his hooded sweat top, a torch and put them in his backpack. He told Mary he needed to go for a walk to have a break from the girl's noise, which she wanted to go and tell them to quieting down but James said that it was ok he could do with the fresh air and not to worry he wouldn't be long.

James headed down to the harbour to where his dingy sat, he had had the boat since he was ten years old it was a present on his birthday from his dad and had lessons on handling the boat. He did not go out very far, just far enough not to hear the noise from the town. Tonight was no different he had his fishing gear with him and hoped to catch at least one, he cast his line and waited. He checked he had every thing he needed it was all here in the boat now he just had to wait. Tonight the moon was full and it shone one the water like a super trouper fixed on the stage waiting on the performance to begin. He did not have long to wait soon the line tugged and James expertly reeled the fish in. Gently removed the hook from its mouth then he bit into the fish it was still alive but he needed the blood from the fish whilst it was still living he hurriedly ate all the fish. Not long now he removed his jeans and shirt, he could feel the change beginning; soon he was finding it hard to breathe and the time being right he plunged into the water, it felt good, he swam under the water around the rocks, lay at the bottom of the seabed. For thirty minutes he became a fish, he did not change into a fish. He was able to swim under the water without the need to breathe air. It was exciting he did not need air as he did on land he did not really know how it worked. He had found out by accident one night not long after his brother beat him he was out in the dinghy fishing, he became hungry and didn't want to return home. He decided to eat one of the fish that he had caught. After all, it could not be that bad the Japanese ate raw fish they called it sushi. He remembered his parents eating it at a very posh hotel when they were on a holiday once. He was not very keen then and he had some doubts now. He could go back home and hope that Jack was not there or he could stay here in the dingy where he was safe, and eat the raw fish. He ate the fish, at first he thought he would be sick but he was so hungry that he over came that feeling. Once he started, it was not that bad and found himself quite enjoying his meal. He was nearly finished when he thought he was choking on a bone, panicking at his inability to breathe he tried to get the dinghy motor started he fell into the water, at first he panicked as the cold sea water dragged him down, shock making him unable to think straight as he sunk to the bottom. He was holding his breath and franticly trying to get back to the surface his lungs crying out for air he could feel his heart pounding in his chest he thought that he was going to die. Unable to hold his breath any longer, he opened his mouth and the salty water rushed into his mouth he could feel his body relaxing he thought that he was dead. However, he could still feel his heart beating. Pounding in his chest after the panic, he had just suffered. He was not being dragged to the bottom of the seabed any more but he was floating there was no panic either he felt so relaxed. He started to swim. Forcing the water out of his mouth then taking another mouthful, he swam around repeating the procedure hi managed to swim around under the water for about ten minutes. Then he felt his body change he felt the need for air he headed back to the surface. As he broke the surface of the water he breathed normally again. Treading the water, he tried to understand what had happened if it was not the fact he was in the water fully clothed he might have thought that it all had been a dream. Then as he swam to the dingy, he realized that this was not normal that this was strange. Should he tell anyone? He had enough to worry about without people thinking that he was a freak.

From the hilltop the man watched the going on below although it was dark he could see the boy in the boat and watched him plunge into the water that was twenty minutes ago he didn't alert any one because he knew who the boy was. He waited till he surfaced., pulled the collar of his long black leather jacket straightened his hat then walked into the night knowing he had found the boy at last.

James loved this feeling, in the water he forgot about all the troubles he had whilst on the land he forgot about his parents and his older brother he forgot about his job in the coffee shop and school,; here nothing he had no worries: and was very happy with that. He could swim with the fish, chase hermit crabs watch jellyfish float past they all had one thing in common nothing seemed to worry them. He swam down to the seabed and lay flat on his back looking up through the water to the surface watching shoals of small fish dart back and forth feeding on plankton. He then turned over and swan to nearby rocks he watched the crabs scurrying under the rocks or bury them under the sand for safety when he swam past. He explored the rocks watched the seaweed moving back and forth with the tides movement. He picked up shells looking inside them for hermit crabs, he found a couple of nice unbroken shells and decided to take them home for the twins, they loved to put them to their ears and listen to the noise it sounded just like the waves breaking on the shore.

Soon he felt the change starting his swimming slowed he could feel the drag of his body as he tried to get to the waters surface. Kicking his leg as hard as he could he surfaced from his watery heaven and gasped the cool night air. filling his lungs with air that they had been screaming out forWhen he could feel the change starting James would wait as long as possible before returning to the stress and worry that waited for him above the waves. He was a short distance from the dingy and had to swim he was tired by the time he pulled himself into the dingy and lay on the floor of the boat staring up at the stars. He wondered why he was able to breathe under the water after eating the raw fish. No way could he tell any one it had to be his secret. Soon he wondered if it was just when he ate raw fish. What would happen if he ate other raw types of meat? Would they have the same effect? He also wondered how many he would have to eat to swim to the Indian Ocean. He was brought back to the moment by his body shivering, he dressed quickly put on the hooded sweat top started the dingy engine and headed towards the orangey glowing lights of the town. Once in to the harbour James tied up the boat checked the time he'd been gone for about an hour and a half not to long to worry Mary it was about the usual time he would take on his walks, he picked up his back pack and set of home.

Chapter 7

James could see the police car sitting in the drive and he sprinted as fast as he could the rest of the way home, when he turned into the drive could see his older brother Jack's car was there also. His heart pounded what were the police doing here. It had been a while since the had came round., no new evidence was what the told Jack the last time they came round the words no new evidence was misleading the had no evidence. James busts through the door shouting for Mary, she appeared from the kitchen and ushered him into the lounge where Jack and his sisters were waiting. He could tell by the scowl Jack threw at him when he appeared in the doorway that Jack was not impressed he had not been around and that the police would not start without him. A police officer led him to a chair beside his sisters of which he was glad as his brother still glowered at him. This made James very uncomfortable. He listened to a police officer talk about how the case about the disappearance of their parents was on going, reviewed the case recently, and had uncovered new evidence and acting on this evidence had recovered their car. Their car, had found at the bottom of a lake. North of the hotel where they had stayed at when they had attended the funeral. However, unfortunately their bodies were not there. The forensics was looking at the car to see if they could get any more evidence and they would keep them posted. James kept his head bowed looking at the floor only once did he move his head or rather his eyes and that was to look at Jack for a brief moment to his surprise Jack held a look of disbelief and was sure he was shaking his head. Had he changed his mind about what he had thought, about them returning home one day James was surprised with his brothers actions but was not going to approach him about anything. The news about the car gave some hope either to find them alive or to find the bodies and let the family grieve. Jack was talking to the police and that gave James a chance to slip out of the room and find Mary. He knew that he was safe when Mary was nearby she stop Jack hurt him. James found Mary in the kitchen and told her the police were here for and what they said. When she asked how he felt about the news he replied; I still think that we will never see them again I do not know why but I feel that they have died. She had a soft spot for James and knew his life had not been easy she also admired the grown up way he was around the twins. An old man's head on young shoulders was what she often said to him.

Jack decided that tonight he was going to stay at the house; he wanted to find out where James had been Mary had only said he went for a walk then she phoned the parents of the twin's friends to collect them due to unforeseen circumstances and arranged for them to have a sleepover later on.

"Did you catch anything" jack asked.

"No" James lied not tonight.

Then Jack said that he was going to go and read the twins a bedtime story then he turned to James and gave him a smile one like the one he used to when they had happier times.

James returned the gesture with a cautious look.

James stood on the porch looking down the drive past Jack's flashy car, past the gates and out to the sea he thought of the difference between here and his secret life beneath the water of the bay in front of him.

It was the Sunday and Jack had been at the house since the police called about the finding of their parent's car but there was no evidence found in or on the car that would enlighten them to their parent's disappearance. James needed to be alone. He could not take the boat out due to the rough weather causing huge waves to crash against the shore. He decided to take to the woods on the outskirts of town. He packed his backpack with water; his Swiss army knife some chocolate and his binoculars. Went to tell Mary where he was going.

"When will tea be ready," he asked Mary.

"Around five." she replied.

I think I am going to head up to the woods. I need a walk. Be home in time for tea" James smiled as he headed out the back door.

Chapter 8

The weather was gloomy, grey clouds tumbled along the sky as if the wind was blowing them just like the tumble weed that western films always had. He looked across out to the water and could see the white crested waves being whipped up by the wind that blew in from the sea. He was walking with the wind blowing on his left which soon turned ear red he tilted his head to shield his face from the blustery gusts of wind that made his eyes water. He walked along the path till he came to the car park that started the beginning of the woodland walk to his surprise there were some cars in the car park he expected it to be empty what with the weather being wild. He never paid the cars much attention. If he did, he might have seen the jeep in the far corner and the man in the driver's seat. The same man that spoke to him in the coffee shop, the same man that had watched him dive into the water on many occasions and not come up for air for at least thirty minutes. He went through the gate that had a big notice board showing the different walks and information on different animals and plants in the area along with the country code a notice about a coffee morning to raise funds to help repair the church roof. James knew the wood his mother used to take him and Jack up here on picnics he remembered the fun he had as he tried to catch Jack as they ran between the trees pretended to be part of Robin Hood's band of merry men or they were heroes fighting off monsters and ogres. When they were older the learned to identify different birds and the different animals by the imprints left on the ground as they went about their way. Today, James subconsciously looked at the ground looking for footprints. He saw dog paw prints in many different sizes, many paw prints left by rabbits, further into the walk he came across deer hoof prints. This sent a wave of excitement through James. He liked to see the deer he loved the way they were so graceful when running across the moor. The other side of the woods, where he was heading now The wind had died down and although the treetops were still being moved by the wind it was considerably less which brought comfort to James as he wasn't keen on the high winds. When he reached the edge of the woods, he stood just inside the trees. Took out his binoculars and scanned the open moor in front of him, slowly he scanned the land from left to right then back again, nothing.He stood a while pondering the idea of going further across the moor. Looking to the sky, he could see the clouds had broken up and patches of blue appeared. He checked his watch and still had plenty of time before tea. Go on he decided he would head for the bushes and there he would be camouflaged. It took James a while to reach the bushed area, there was no track to follow and the rough ground made it quite tiring. He found a dip in the ground in which when he lay in it he was well hidden. He waited. Scanning the horizon for any sighting of deer, he waited but nothing. Closing his eyes, he let his ears do the looking. He could hear the wind as it swept across the moor. A crow making a noise about something Then he heard nothing, sleep overtook him, as he lay hidden from the world.

James was suddenly wakened the crack from the shotgun rudely rousing him from the sleep that had overtaken him. For a split second he froze, the shock rendered him senseless, trying to collect his senses he heard men declaring a good shot. Looking up from the hollow in which he lay he saw two men about one hundred and fifty yards to his left walking across the moor. He raised his binoculars and followed their track. They walked on for about ten minutes, then crouched down in the long grass and busied themselves. Out off sight from James's view he could only imagine what they were doing, but he had a good idea the men were poachers and by the time they were spending crouched hidden in the long grass, they had killed a deer. They would have to remove the innards because the deer produces a poison that would make the meat useless.

On the edge of the woods, the man with the long leather coat watched. He followed James through the woods keeping a safe distance from him he did not want to be seen by the boy the time was not right not at the moment. He knew that this boy was the one he was looking for, but it was too soon.

He had stopped in the car park to eat lunch and read the local newspaper looking for a job, he would need one but not just any thing he needed a special one. He now stood watching the poachers as they cleaned the deer. He switched between watching them and to where James laid, the men left with the deer wrapped up in several bags after having carved the best cuts of meat. He saw James leave the hollow and go to where the poachers had been he felt a sense of excitement as he saw the boy kneel down at the spot.

James saw the gory mess left by the poachers. He felt anger at first he thought deer were wonderful animals how could anyone do that leave the leftovers just lying there.

Then he wondered what would happen if he were to eat a piece of raw meat would he be able to run as fast and as gracefully as the deer did. He pondered the idea. He thought back to when he was in the water how he loved the sense of peace and tranquillity; in the water, he had no worries as he swam along side the shoals of fish. He loved the way crabs never scurried away from him. The way the jellyfish dangled weightless floating past. He liked the way his body eased through the water with no drag. Then his thoughts changed to the deer how they moved with speed and sure footed as they crossed the moor, Taking his Swiss Army Knife from his pocket, he looked at the leftovers to find a piece of the bloody meat that he could eat. Finding a suitable piece, he held it in his hand debating with himself whether to eat it.

The man on the edge of the wood silently urged him to eat, wanting to see the results. The fish thing was one thing but he prayed that he would see something more exciting.

James looked around he saw nothing. He strained his ears all he could hear was the pounding in his ears from his own heart beating. He doubled checked no one. The worst thing he thought was that someone saw him. How would he explain? James ate the chunk of raw meat. It was not that bad. He felt no change. Perhaps it had not been enough. Maybe he needed to eat more. He looked down at the carcase to see if there was another suitable piece when he felt the urge to run. He ran head on to the wind not to fast to start with. He looked all around to see if anyone was there. This was fun to feel free the way the deer had. To run sure footed over the rough terrain. He ran faster sure that he was alone. He could feel the wind blowing against his skin, blowing through his hair. He ran faster than he could ever imagine he was not even out of breath. His senses were more extreme than ever, he could smell the grass it smelt sweet just like it had just been mowed the peaty earth filled his nostrils, the scent of a fox came to him quite strong indicating that it was quite close. He was not frightened; the fox was more likely to be afraid of him. That made him wonder would he have the scent of a human, which he looked like, or a deer. If the fox thought he was a deer, would it be confused? Maybe the fox would think he was going mad. The thought amused James immensely so much, so that he burst out laughing. He laughed so hard that his sides ached; it had been a long time since he had had a good laugh.

He felt happy. His senses were still alert he started to run again wanting to keep this feeling he had, the happiness and the change that took place when he had ate the raw meat a little longer. He was heading to the woods still running as fast as the deer when he started to feel the change he decided that he would try to jump the fence with the agility of the deer before he returned to plain old James. Just short of the fence, one stride. Too late, he changes. To late to stop himself He was going to fast. He tried to clear the fence but caught his foot on the wire and crashed to the ground, luckily, no bones were broken but he has a nasty gash on his leg. Quickly he removed his backpack and pulled out paper tissues to stem the blood from his cut. Panic was starting to set in how he was going to get home. Would he die? He thought he heard someone shout his name. He listened again had he imagined it. No, there it was again it was his brother Jack. Was he going to be on the receiving end of abuse from him because he had been told go and to find him? Should he keep quiet and wait until he had gone? Alternatively, take a chance, looking down at his leg he knew he had to take a chance.

"Over here" yelled James "I am hurt help"

Soon Jack was at his side ready to help James. Jack picked up the backpack, took out more tissues and pressed them down on James's leg eventually the bleeding had stopped then he removed his shirt and tore a strip big enough to make a tourniquet for James's leg. Once he had done that, he put James's backpack over his shoulder and carefully helped James to his feet. It took them ages to get back to the car park, which was empty apart from Jack's sports car, which was a welcome sight as far as James was concerned.

Chapter 9

The man with the leather jacket had seen everything and felt very pleased with what he had witnessed, he saw James eat the raw deer meat and watched as he ran over the moor at great speed he then knew that this was the boy what he had been looking for. All the trouble that he had gone to did what he had done, and covers his track every thing was going to be worth it in the end. Watching from his vantage point he was himself already trying to figure out how to get the boy's DNA. When he saw the boy trying to jump the fence and fall he had to stop himself from going over. At first, he thought he had seriously injured himself but then saw the boy move he waited to see if he was going to get up. He was about to go over to the boy when he heard the shouts from his brother. He watched as he helped him and got him to his feet. When they were out of sight, he went over to where the two boys had been. He saw the bloodied tissues left behind. How he thought his luck had changed. The day started well. He was not intending watching the boy, he was more concerned about finding a suitably job nearby. He had gone to the car park to search the paper and have a bite to eat, he was about to leave when he spotted the boy walking through the car park. He decided to follow out of curiosity. Now he was glad he did because not only had he witnessed what happened to the boy when he ate the raw deer meat but saw the changes in his ability to copy the deer. When he saw the boy in the water, he could not be certain that he was actually breathing under the water he could only assume; now he knew one hundred percent this was the boy. Now the bloodied tissues that he was putting into a bag should have the boy's DNA on them. With no time to waste, he headed back to the car park he took a different path back as he did not want the boys to see him Once he reached the jeep, he wasted no time starting the vehicle and headed the twenty five miles back to the lab.

Once the boys were in the car and James was as comfortable as possible Jack headed to the private clinic, which the family had used long before the boys were born. Jack pulled up at the main door and ordered James to wait there until he got help. He was back in no time with a porter and helped James on to the trolley. I will be with you once I have parked the car, will not be long. James could hear the roar of Jacks car as the porter wheeled James in to the clinic. He wondered if Jack would come back or leave him here. The doctor came in to attend to James at the same time as Jack. The doctor had been the family doctor for twenty years and he knew both boys very well. As he examined James's leg, he had the look of concern, he turned and asked Jack if he wanted to let Mary knew about the accident he could use the phone at the reception desk. When Jack left, the doctor started to ask James where he had been at the time of the accident. Was there any one or any thing else involved? How did he feel just before it happened? How was he feeling now? All the time he was questioning James he poked and prodded at the gapping wound in James's leg.

James answered the questions... with a slight hesitance. Should he mention about the raw fish, the raw meat, and the changes that occurred, would he laugh at him or think he had gone crazy? He thought against it and answered the questions with lies.

When Jack appeared, the doctor told them that James would need to have the leg stitched and cleaned and would need to have an operation and that Jack would need to bring Mary here, as she would need to sigh a consent form.

Mary was shocked to here the news about James. It was only a few hours since he left the house, and now he was in the clinic waiting to undergo surgery. Hurriedly she gathered a few things together and met Jack and the twins in the drive. The twins squashed in the back and Mary in the front Jack drove in silence back to the clinic.

When they arrived, they saw the doctor waiting at the front door, fearing the worst they hurried over to see if there was a problem. Mary could already feel her insides churning and she tried to hold back the tears by telling herself that she had to be strong for the twins and Jack. they had been led to the room that James was in It was a big room that was painted white there were pale green curtains closed over a large window and the bed covers were matching the curtains. I n the corner was a wash hand basin with big fluffy towels hanging on a rail beside it. The bed looked huge with James's small body laying in it. He had been giving a sedative and was a bit drowsy but managed to call for Mary. He said that he was sorry for all the trouble he had caused. Mary told him that he had nothing to be sorry for and that he was going to be all right. She was holding his hand and stroking his hair. Soon the sedative overtook him and he drifted of to sleep.

As the doctor prepared James for the surgery he handed the nurse a blood sample for the lab to check, as she left the doctor took a sample from James and put it in his pocket. Then he took a piece of tissue from the wound put it in a test tube and placed that in his pocket along with the blood sample.

When James came round Mary was there alone. She sent Jack home with the twins. James was a bit groggy and he called out for his mum he remembered her she was there before he fell asleep she was stroking his hair and holding his hand as she did when he had been ill before. Again, he cried out for her. He could hear a voice speaking to him but it was not his mum. He felt a hand holding his, a warm hand he also felt the hand stroking his hair He was about to call again when he remembered they were gone, he missed his mum. He never told anyone how much he did but just now, he would give anything for to have her here holding his hand and stroking his hair. He opened his eyes and stared at the ceiling. He could hear Mary talking to him trying to comfort him. He felt so alone. His thoughts wandered to the Indian Ocean he tried to imagine the white sands. The palm trees as they swayed in the tropical breeze the blue sea. Soon sleep had taken over again.

Chapter 10

The jeep turned in to the car park of a new purpose built building with large smoke glass windows that made it look like a large black dice. The building was home to the most up to date forensic unit for miles around and was being used both the by the police and medical students. It was very different from the old unit where he first worked, where he first learned about the boy. The man got out the jeep and headed to the main entrance. Checking that he had the boys bloodied tissues; he then went through the revolving doors and was meet by the security guard. Graham did not want the guard to hold him up any longer than. He said his goodbyes and headed to the lift. The security guard greeted him as he walked passed him then remembered that there was a message from Doctor Newbury for him; he did not expect to see him tonight.

"Mr Greenlaw I have a message for you" he called after him.

"I didn't expect you in tonight sir," he said as he waved a piece of paper in the air.

Mr Greenlaw turned and walked back over to the guard. Took the piece and replied "I have some work that I needed finished by tomorrow afternoon, but would not be late" he said as he headed back to the lift.

He read the message from Dr Newbury it was not that important just wanting to know if he was free next weekend to have a round of golf. He would phone him in the morning, he needed to be quick before to samples he had would be no good. He swiped his security card through the device on the door gave a peep let him know the door was now unlocked. He opened the door, the lights came on automatically they were bright, and Mr Greenlaw had to blink a few times to let his eyes adjust. The room was a large open planned, there was many glass-fronted cupboards, which was home to an array of bottles. Most were brown; they were come in all sorts of sizes. All contained chemicals that had strange Latin names. The room was spotless every thing had been put away. There was also a strong smell of disinfectant. Normally he did not smell the disinfectant but tonight it was a strong smell, indicating that the cleaners had not long left, which was a good thing because he was less likely to be disturbed. He wasted no time in getting started, he did not want arouse suspicion.

Using a cotton bud and a saline solution, he managed to get a sample of blood to test.

After Dr Newbury had attended to James, he hurried to the basement where there was a lab. It wasn't a big sophisticated lab just a lab to cater for health checks from the clinic anything major was sent to bigger labs at the local hospital. However, there was everything Dr Newbury needed.

James had fallen into a peaceful asleep, which was a relief to Mary, she was worried when James had came back to the side room as he was very restless almost delirious, calling out for his mum, going on about the deer and poachers and being shot. So much so, she was beginning to think that he was the one to have been shot she rang for the nurse who came in almost immediately. She took James temperature then paged the doctor. Dr Newbury came in and the nurse spoke to him he replied and sent her to get antibiotics and a fan to try to get his temperature down. When the nurse had, left Dr Newbury asked what James was trying to say Mary had repeated what James had said and told the doctor her fears about him being shotDr Newbury told Mary that he found no evidence that he had been shot and the wound was definitely a tear possibly the cause was barbed wire. He then assured her that James was going to be fine. The nurse came in with a syringe and the fan; the Doctor injected James with the antibiotic whilst the nurse plugged the fan on and positioned it to give James a cooling breeze. They both left at the same time and told Mary not to hesitate and buzz them at anytime. About five minutes later the nurse returned with a welcoming cup of coffee. The gesture brought a smile to Mary's face; the nurse asked if there was anything else, she could do. Mary asked if she could use the phone to let them at home know how James was and to make sure that Jack was managing the twins okay. The nurse showed Mary where the phone was and said that she would wait with James until she came back.

The nurse checked James's temperature and was relieved that it had started to come down, and then she straightened the covers up and waited on Mary's return. When Mary returned she could see that James was more comfortable which eased her mind. The nurse told her that his temperature was coming down and he would be less agitated when he woke up. The relief was too much for Mary she sat down beside the bed and cried.

Dr Newbury took the test tube containing James's blood sample and the test tube with the muscle tissue and started to analyse the samples. First, he analysed the blood, he compared it to information that he had in James's medical file and it was the same, which brought slight relief. Next he checked the muscle tissue, all the tests came back that there was no change to James's DNA or his genetic make up. Unlike the tests, that Mr Greenlaw carried out.

James woke up as the nurse opened the curtains and let the morning sun stream through the window, it immediately that cheered James up. He blinked his eyes to help them adjust to the sunlight. He stretched. Yawned and tried to sit up. He noticed Mary sleeping in the chair. The nurse came over to help him sit up. She asked if he was okay, and did he need any painkillers. He said he was a bit sore but did not need any painkillers but would like a drink. She left the room to get a drink and to let Dr Newbury that James was awake. When she returned, she brought a mug of tea and plate of toast and a mug of coffee for Mary, who was sitting beside James and Dr Newbury she placed the tray down and left the room.

Dr Newbury was chatting to James trying to ascertain exactly what had happened to James. He fired questions at James in as subtle a very as possible not to alarm either James or Mary. However, there was underlying concern on the doctor's part. At some point he was going to have to speak with the boy, but was this the time, he was not sure; the disappearance of the boys parents was very untimely. At first, he thought that he was to blame. He had not meant for things to get as far as they did. He only meant to be a friend for James's mum Andrea she had hit a rough patch in her marriage. He had admired her for a long time she was easy to talk to, and had an air of calm about her she had long straight black hair, which had sheen to it, and she always looked like she had just stepped out of the most expensive hair saloon. She had the figure of a model perfectly proportioned. When she had an appointment to see him he had to be very professional.

Not long after their first baby was born, a girl named Carla she developed a serious infection and after three days Carla died, she was only three months old. At her funeral, most of the town's people were there as the family were quite well known and well respected. The death of Carla was devastating to the family. Dr Newbury thought that Andrea was going to suffer a breakdown. She was so vulnerable, so fragile he would have done any thing to stop her suffering. One day she had come to see him. As she walked to the door both of them went to open the door at the same time and their hands touched on the handle. There was a moment of electric magnetism between them as the looked at each other. Their eyes locked on each other neither moved. it was like they had been completely frozen in timeWhen Andrea leaned over to him and kissed him, not a peck but a passionate kiss that for a split second left him paralysed but only for a split second then he returned the gesture. The ringing of his phone interrupted them. He was about to apologize when she gave him a peck on the cheek, opened the door and parted "meet me at the city library tomorrow at 1.00"she said just before she closed the door leaving him standing there open mouthed, alone with the phone ringing.

Chapter 11

He went to the city library the next day he felt like an awkward gawky teenager that was going on his first date unsure of what was in store for him. On one hand, he was excited and looking forward to this encounter. On the other hand nervous because his future could be down the tubes if anyone found out what had and was going on. As he waited, he looked at the biology section he picked up a book on genetics, opened it up, and started to read. He knew almost everything that was in this book, this was is his field. He had been interested in this field for as long as he could remember. As a little boy, he would ask his father questions about how was a boy a made a boy, how did twins look alike. His father had been a scientist working on cures for all kinds of diseases. He admired him and wanted to follow his example. He went to university studied hard and with a degree in Forensics and set up a forensic lab, helping the police solve murders. Once his father died, he decided that he would like to go back to university to study medicine and become a doctor.

A noise brought him back to the present. Turning round he saw Andrea waiting at the table, which stood in the middle of the room, she was smiling at him, and he walked over and sat opposite her. Nervously he looked around to see if the were alone. He was about to ask her how she was feeling when she spoke

"I hope you're not angry with me? I could not help it; I will not tell anyone if you do not. If you want, I will change doctors"

He looked at her and knew that she had reconsidered. He was slightly disappointed he would, if circumstances were different and Andrea was not married he would certainly pursue this woman but he was her doctor and she was married, also this vulnerable woman had not long lost her first child. He had to let her go. He looked at her and shook his head.

"Do not be carried away with yourself, you are under a lot of stress now lets look at it as a moment of madness" and gave her a smile which she returned.

"What book are you reading? She asked him she sounded genuinely interested.

"Oh just some boring stuff all about genetics I don't think it will interest you" he replied.

"Excuse the pun, but do not judge a book by its cover," retorted Andrea. Do you think that all I do all day is housework? Maybe I have studied medicine or biology somewhere.

"I'm sorry I didn't mean it like that" he quickly tried to backtrack "do you have any interests in medical issues or genetics.

"No" she replied with the slightest hint of a smile. "Just teasing been to busy with the house and the business. Nevertheless, with the entire break through in modern technology and this new forensics it all sounds quite intriguing".

They chatted some more mostly about every day things. How things were in the world and what they would change to make the world right. Dr Newbury glanced up at the clock and realised that the two of them had been chatting for two hours "Would you like to go somewhere and get a bite to eat" he asked her.

She suggested that they went to one of their coffee shops and she would treat him to some home made baking. They decided to go to the one her husband Julian was working at just in case they had seen together and tongues wagged. Andrea went to pick up a few books, Dr Newbury collected a few more medical books, and they met out side. They decided to say that they met at the library. He agreed gave her a hug, he could smell her perfume. It was a floral smell. He would remember that aroma for a long time. When they parted, he caught a glimpse of her and by her looks, he thought that he enjoyed that encounter as much as he had himself. They walked over to the car park and each got into their respective vehicles. Doctor Newbury drove his car behind Andrea with a slight feeling of rejection. He had been awake the whole night before turning over in his mind what had happened at the clinic the day before. How she kissed him first and how much passion came from it. How she responded to his kiss. What might have happened if the phone had not rung? Perhaps the phone ringing was blessing. Who knows what might have happened. Then he started to think what mess things would turn out if things had gone further, a marriage break up, the publicity as people found, out his job, his future, the clinic which he had taken over two years ago and was now well established he would lose the lot. Coming to his senses, he gave a heavy sigh and thanked god for the phone that rung.

They reached the coffee shop and managed to find a space to park the cars. He got out of his car first locked then pause, unsure if he should walk over to help Andrea. Just as he decided that, it was a courteous thing to do and headed to Andrea's car to offer his assistance she opened the car and waved for him to just go on ahead. He declined the suggestion and instead he went over to her car to see if she needed a hand with any thing.

After that incident, things were a little strange for a while, but after a few months, everything was back to normal.

Chapter 12

There was a knock at the door and Dr Newbury called for the person to come in. the door opened to reveal the nurse trying to manoeuvre a trolley through the door. Dr Newbury went over to assist her. Turning to James and saying that he was going to check the wound. To see if there was any sigh of any infection and if the stitches were okay he might send him home. If he promised to have complete rest unnecessary walking In addition, if, turning to Mary said "if there in any change whatsoever he was to come right back".

Both James and Mary nodded and agreed. Dr Newbury would rather have kept James in as he needed to speak with him but did not will not to cause any suspicion. As he started to remove the bandages, he secretly hoped that there was a reason to keep James in.James prayed that there was nothing wrong. Perhaps Dr Newbury should have prayed rather than hoped as James's leg showed no sign of infection and the stitches were all present and correct there was not even much swelling. James looked down at the wound on his leg and his face drained of colour he didn't realise that his leg was so badly cut, he could feel himself getting light headed and his stomach turn he thought that he was going to be sick, Mary seen this and put her arm around his shoulders and tried to comfort him. The doctor noticed this and asked him if he was all right. James could not answer him because he was concentrating on breathing and trying to stop himself from passing out. Dr Newbury quickly covered James's leg and attended to James he handing him a glass of water then tried to assure him that although it looked bad it would heal and he would not have any physical problems with his leg and if there was a lot of scarring and it caused him concern there was always cosmetic surgery. James took a couple of minutes to get himself together then said that he was alright now and that he had not expected it to be so bad, and that the doctor could start to replace the bandages.

Mary went with the nurse to phone the house to ask if Jack could pick them up as the doctor was allowing James home as long as he rested. Jack said that he would be there in about thirty minutes. He got the neighbour to come and stay with the twins who were still at home as they refused to go to school until James came home. Emma and Sarah been up early but had stayed in their room busying themselves making get well soon cards for James. When Jack popped his head round the door to let them know that he was going to the clinic to pick up James and Mary and that their neighbour was going to stay with them till they came back the girls smile said that they were pleased then they asked if they could put up banners to welcome James back. Jack was about to say that James had only been gone overnight not months but stopped himself as he knew that a statement like that might upset them as it was now four months since their parents disappearance. He looked at them with their eager faces willing him to say yes. It worked he said they could but only if Mrs Gurley was willing to hang the banners as he didn't want them to be climbing up ladders, one invalid was enough.

Jack pulled his car up in front of the clinic and hurried inside, James was in a wheelchair, waiting at the front doors whilst Mary followed with his belongings and a pair of crutches.Suddenly he realised that his sports car would not be big enough. Feeling a bit awkward he approached Dr Newbury to tell him about the predicament that he was in but Dr Newbury solved the problem, he was going their way, he would take the wheelchair and James in his car, and Mary could go with Jack. They were all loaded up and Dr Newbury followed Jack's car. He chatted to James as they drove mainly asking him how things were, was there any news about his parents. How was school what subjects he was good at and how were the twins. James replied all his questions then James asked if he had any things he liked to do when he was not working. He replied that he used to do a bit of gardening and that he played golf and liked to fish. James told the doctor that he also liked to fish and he invited the doctor to join him once he was more mobile.

"Sounds like a good idea I accept the offer" replied the doctor. Then as they were approaching James's house he asked how Jack had been he told him that he knew about the beating he had given by him. James stared out of the window unwilling to speak; he was unsure what to say in case Jack found out and gave him another beating. But this was a doctor and he knew that he shouldn't repeat whatever James told him, clearing his throat he told him that Jack hadn't beat him since that first attack on him but several times he had scared him because of his temper and that he tried to keep well out of his way. However, he had over the past few weeks, ever since the police had found their parents car showed signs of the old Jack. "He was strange," James, said "hard figure out. He was up and down like a fiddlers elbow" James heard the doctor give a short burst of laughter at his last comment.

That was one of his mum's sayings. James turned and looked at the doctor and he gave a smile he knew that he could trust him and one day he would be able to speak to him about his ability to breathe underwater and what happened on the moor when he ate raw meat. As they turned into the drive, they noticed the banners welcoming James home. "Someone has been missed," said Dr Newbury then he turned to James and said, "My door is always open if you need to talk or just want advice".

Once they got James settled in Mary offered Dr Newbury a coffee but he declined saying that he needed to attend to some business, but thanks, anyway he said as he headed to the door and reminded James that he was to rest.

Chapter 13

Dr Newbury headed to the golf course he received a telephone call from Mr Greenlaw to say that he would take him up on his offer to a round of golf. Dr Newbury had known Mr Geenlaw's father Stuart they had met at university and managed to get work together in the same laboratories. Stuart was women man and quite often had two women on the go at once. He said that he would never settle down he did not want to be tied to one woman. Stuart studied hard and played even harder. If Stuart thought that any of the women were getting to serious, they would find themselves dumped. Then he would find someone else.

He was never to careful, that is how Graham Greenlaw the young man he was going to meet came to be. Dr Newbury was working in the lab with when Stuart came in he looked as if he had just seen a ghost; he walked over to him and asked if he could have a word. That is when the story of Graham unfolded. It seamed that one of the women that Stuart has dumped was pregnant he did not want to marry the woman and certainly did not want the responsibility of a child. He asked Dr Newbury for some advice. However, Dr Newbury's advice was not what he wanted to hear, as Dr Newbury believed in doing the right thing but Stuart was not having any of that. He later found out that Stuart had met with the woman and paid her a lot of money to get rid of it. Neither of them heard from the woman again.

Seventeen years later Graham Greenlaw appeared at the lab. Stuart knew straight away, who he was. He was his double. For about five minutes, the three men stood speechless. Dr Newbury was the first to speak when he asked if any one wanted coffee. Stuart cleared his throat and nodded blinking a few times but not taking his eyes of this young man. Dr Newbury then turned to the young man and asked if he would like a coffee. The young man nodded but he never took his eyes of his father. Dr Newbury left the two of them, went to the kitchen area, and made the coffees. He could hear their voices but could not make out what they were saying. He smiled to himself after all these years thinking that the woman had got rid of the unborn child he turned up on the doorstep. When he returned with the coffees, he could tell by their body language that things a bit tense. Should he offer to help each other or let Stuart deal with it himself? Looking at Stuarts face, he thought he should offer to help his friend. The offer of his help was accepted. He introduced himself to the young man, asked if he was okay with his presence being there, and held out his hand to the young man. The young man accepted the doctor's hand and introduced himself as Graham Greenlaw. Then the three of them sat round the small coffee table to discuss the past and the future.

Stuart was in shock he could hardly talk. What information did this man have? A man who he knew was his son a person that he knew nothing about. Know about him. Did he know that he had not wanted him and that he had paid his mother to get rid of him? Where this woman was now was she still alive. God he could not even remember her name. He had heard nothing from her since he gave her the money. He presumed that she had got rid of their unborn child and that she moved on.He had. Now his world had been blown to pieces He watched the young man in front of him he tried to feel something for him he after all was his son. A son he never knew existed how he wished that he could turn the clock back. He would have made sure that she had got rid of it. He would have gone with her. Now he was sitting face to face with a stranger, a stranger that was his son. What was he going to do? He sat there in a daze. He could hear the other two talking but it did not make any sense. His head was swimming his pulse was pounding in his ears. He felt sick. Dr Newbury shook Stuart's arm and brought him back to the here and now. Stuart looked at Graham and shook his head. Graham spoke he told his father that his mother had been ill and when she was on her deathbed, she told him the truth about his father. She told him that he was a scientist and that he did not know anything about him. He said that as a child, he had asked about him but she denied that she knew who he was saying that a stranger had raped her whilst she was drunk at a party. He was not to ask any more about it as it brought back terrible memories. As he did not like to see her upset, he decided that he would never speak about it to her again.

Relief came to Stuart when he heard the story at least he would not know that he had paid to have him aborted.

Graham went on to talk about his childhood he lived most of his life and motels alone whilst his mother worked through the day as waitress and worked the bars at night. Sometimes she would bring clients back to their room. Then his mother would be throw hen out on the street until they were finished or if he were asleep, they would do it in the room beside him. He had not doing too well at school his grades were low and he had constantly bullied. However, when he went to high school he realised that if he wanted to get anywhere in life get out of the hole he was in he would have to knuckle down study hard it was then he changed. It was not easy but the determination to make something of his life pushed him on.

Stuart listened and he tried to imagine what it must have been like for him as time went on Stuart began to feel guilty about his actions in the past maybe he could help now, if he was homeless, he could let him stay with him. He asked Graham what he had doing with himself. Was he was working or if he was at collage? He was at college studying science and biology he replied he was at the City College, which was about forty miles from here, and he stayed in the halls. He asked how long had it been since his mother had passed away. He replied that it was two months. He had traced Stuart. That he had found him last week but was not sure about meeting him but he had only plucked up the courage to come in today.

Dr Newbury watched and listened, he was not sure about what he was hearing, the more he heard the more suspicious he became of Graham. He watched, as the two of them as they spoke and he noted the change in Stuart, had believed in all Graham's stories.

When Graham had left, Stuart asked Dr Newbury if there was any thing that they could let Graham do in the lab when he was not at college and the weekends so that he could be earning some money. We will talk about it in the morning as it was getting late.

At home, Dr Newbury made a few phone calls. He had contacts at the college. He certainly was not going to jump into anything without speaking to his contacts.

The ringing of the phone had abruptly awoken Doctor Newbury. The phone's loud ring was deafening him. He fumbled with the light.He checked the time. It was still dark and the clock's numbers glowed like a bright neon light informing him that it was only four thirty. Who would be phoning him at this time in the morning? He picked up the receiver to find out who was on the other end. He was about to speak in an anything but pleasant tone when the man on the other end spoke first. Dr Newbury its Tony from the City College been doing these checks that you asked for, the checks on Mr Graham Greenlaw.

He forgot for a moment that he had asked Tony to check up on Greenlaw. Yes, he managed to say what did you managed to find out.

Tony replied that it seems that Mr Greenlaw just managed to pass the entrance exams. He also is not Mr Greenlaw. He had changed his name just after he had started the course. His real name is Barry Watson. He who also had a police record, which included theft, and violence the most recent was an assault on his mother she was hospitalised for two weeks. It was touch and go. However, she pulled through had pressed charges against him. She also has an injunction on him so that he cannot contact her. He cannot come within a mile of her neitherHe seemed like a very nasty person.

"Do you have an address for his mother" Dr Newbury Asked?

Tony gave him the address that was on his file but said he did not know if she would still be there. It was a start. He would check it out in the morning he told Tony.

Tony apologized for calling so late but it took him longer than he thought. Then with a click, the phone went dead. Dr Newbury smiled at this because for as long as he had known Tony he never heard him say goodbye over the phone. He replaced the receiver then layback down to go back to sleep but his mind was to awake. He headed to the kitchen clicked the kettle then headed for the shower.

Stuart was already in the lab when Dr Newbury when he arrived later that morning.

He had gone to the address that Tony had given him in the early hours of the morning. He parked his car near to the house and waited. He watched to see if there was any one at home. He also noticed that an unmarked police car passed every thirty minutes he decided to leave when one of the occupants of one of the cars slowed down and took his registration. He then headed to the police station to find out if speak to the chief inspector. Another old friend from his university yearsLuck was on his side he was on duty they went into his office and tried to find out more about Barry alias Graham Greenlaw. He also told the chief about being at the house and that he had parked his car near the house and it took two hours before someone noticed him and took his registration. The chief said he would deal with it; they were not too observant that lot and needed a shake up. The two men chatted. Catching up on old the times. He could not tell Dr Newbury anything about the case as it was on going. The chief asked what interested him in Barry. He then told him the story about Stuart being his father and how he did not want the child and how he gave the mother money to get rid of the unborn child. How he had turned up at the lab, and told them that he was at the City College and he only found out about his father on his mothers deathbed. However, he himself had made a few phone calls and found out that his mother was still alive. He was not sure how he was going to tell Stuart. Stuart wanted to give him work at the lab but knowing what he knew now there was no way. The chief agreed that it was not advisable they should wait.

Stuart was making coffee when he went through the door he automatically made one for him. He went over to the kitchen area, took the offered mug, looked Stuart straight in the eye, and said,

"We need to talk." Stuart nodded his head and said, "two minutes, have you had breakfast or would you like one of these" he held up a paper bag for Dr Newbury.

Just before he could ask, what the contents were, Stuart must have read his mind, or perhaps it was the expectant look on his face Stuart announced that it was bacon.

"Two bacon rolls from the burger van".

They used the van quite regularly it was handy as it was in the park across the road from their lab and often they could smell the food cooking through the open windows.

"No thanks been fed already". Stuart smiled subconsciously because he really wanted the two rolls to himself; he had not eaten since yesterday.

Chapter 14

He had went to the City College to see what he could find out about his son as he wasn't taken in by his performance at first yes he had been, but thinking back over the meeting he could see the cracks in his story. He also wondered if Graham knew that he paid his mother to get an abortion. So he headed to the college to find out more.

As the two men sat across from each other sipping at the coffee, each wondered how to put their findings to each other. Stuart spoke first "he isn't who he said he was. His name is Barry Watson. His mother is still alive, he beat her up quite bad and she pressed charges of assault against him His grades are not great either, and the college are close to kicking him out". All the time he was staring into his mug.

As if, there were notes inside the mug telling him what to say? He felt a bit embarrassed and did not want to look Dr Newbury in the eye. He took a drink of coffee unsure what to say or do next. Dr Newbury sensed his discomfort and decided to let him know that he too had been trying to find out more because he also did not believe what Graham was telling them. He could see the relief on Stuart's face it was almost immediate.

"We need to talk to this Graham or Barry, but first we need to figure out what we want and if we decide to give him a chance we need to set rules and make sure they are carried out." Dr Newbury said.

"Yes thank you, I've been worried we've been friends for such a long time and I should have taken your advice all those years ago then perhaps I wouldn't have all this mess." A rather subdued Stuart replied.

"Don't worry we'll get something sorted out. We need to find out what he knows. I think we should talk to his mother do you think you could manage or will I go on my own." Dr Newbury asked.

It took no more than two seconds for Stuart to reply. "If I see that woman I don't think I could control my temper so it would be better if you went on your own." Stuart seemed to be getting flustered so to lighten things a bit Dr Newbury asked if he wanted to know if there was any change from the abortion. That brought a slight smile to Stuart's lips. Dr Newbury finished his coffee walked over to the sink, rinsed out his mug, turned to Stuart and said "no time like the present"

Dr Newbury drove his car to the local florist and got a bunch of flowers made up. Nothing to expensive, he was not that fond of the woman when she was dating Stuart and he did not think she would have changed much. However, he needed an excuse to get to the front door, as he was not sure if the police were patrolling through the day. He parked the car in the next street and walked round to the house. He did not see any sigh of police in the street nor did he notice any unmarked cars patrolling the area. He went up the path to the front door and rang the bell he waited but there was no reply. He was just about to write his phone number on the card when the door opened slightly enough for the woman to peep with one eye round the corner of the door. He introduced himself and asked if he could speak with her. She opened the door further to get a better look and then she remembered who he was.

"Why should I want to speak to you couldn't he come himself. I suppose that little brat has been in touch with him and gave you all a little sob story well" she flung the door open to reveal her battered body. She had a plaster cast on her right arm her face was a mass of bruising, and her nose looked like it had been broken.

"This is his handy work. Nearly killed me he did, I am lucky to be alive. Never have I seen him get so angry he lost it and went berserk." She stood in the door way so that he could see the full extent of her injuries.

"Please let me come in and talk to you," he asked again,

"We Stuart and I has had a visit but we need to know more. We would like to help"

She paused for a moment then stood back and let him in.

He handed the flowers to her. She took them and from her reactions, he reckoned that she was not used to someone being nice to her. She just stared at them. He thought that she was going to start crying but she turned and said that they were lovely and she would put them in a vase. She showed him into the living room and asked him to take a seat. It was a dull room with outdated furniture that none of it matched. An ashtray was full of dog ends. Some had fallen out of the ashtray and burnt the carpet. He could also smell the distinctive smell of dope. The place was an absolute mess the wished that he had stayed outside. The door creaked open and she stood there with the flowers in a vase that looked so out of place in the surrounding squalor. "Would you like a cup of tea," she asked or "something stronger perhaps".

The thought of drinking anything from here turned his stomach.

"No not long finished one" he lied.

He noticed that there were no photographs of Graham, but there were some of another boy. A curly blond haired lad, who looked to be about ten years old in photo, it looked quite a recent picture. The lad looked to be extremely obese.

"If only that Barry had turned out to be like his brother, he used to pick on Mark right from the day he came home from the hospital. He changed when I was expecting he started to play truant from school, also started to shoplift. The police were always bringing him home. Telling me to have more control over him, but he was uncontrollable" she paused for a moment then walking past he Doctor she muttered "I should have got rid it like his father wanted. Maybe he knew what he would turn out like."

Dr Newbury took his chance and asked, "Did you ever tell him that his father paid you to have an abortion?" He stared at the woman as he waited for an answer. However, knowing what he heard and what he saw he already knew the answer.

"Yes" she replied staring back, "that's when he attacked me".

Was he high on drugs the doctor asked?

"No he doesn't take drugs he does not drink either" her hands turned towards her body. "Who smokes the dope?" quizzed the doctor.

"I do being doing it for years". She retorted.

In his mind's eye, he was beginning to get his own picture of how Barry had grown up. A life of neglect, abuse and humiliation and would bet his last pound that he had to look after his brother, who was now used as a trophy against him. Maybe he would have lost it too if he was Barry. He had seen enough he needed to escape into the fresh air outside.

The drive back to the lab was slow due to road works and that gave him time to think. Maybe he had jumped to the wrong conclusion. Maybe he left home to escape the abuse and changed his name to make a new start he took a long breath in and loud and slowly exhaled saying "Oh what a tangled web we weave very tangled indeed".

When he entered the lab, he heard Barry's voice

"I know I said that she was dead and to me she is I never want to see her again that's why I went to college, that's why I changed my name. I am struggling at college but I am trying really trying. I don't have anyone to turn to and I thought that you could help me."

Barry was standing at the desk speaking to his father who looked rather relieved when he saw Dr Newbury come through the door. He walked over to where the two were. He pulled up two chairs and ordered Barry to sit.

"Now young man things are serious and we need to get a few things straight." He said looking Barry who dropped like a stone into the chair.

"Yes "he replied.

"First thing is what do we call you? Barry or Graham" asked Dr Newbury.

"Graham please I'd rather you called me graham" he said looking at Dr Newbury with a puzzled look on his face.

Dr Newbury continued, "You are in a very serious situation, you could be looking at a jail sentence you are also on your way out of college. If you want our help, we need to stop all the lies. You also need to get a social worker who will help with reports for the courts. You will need to get anger management and will attend that's only the start" Dr Newbury stood up went into his wallet brought out a twenty pound note. He asked Graham to go to the burger van in the park across the road and get two bacon rolls for him turning to Stuart. He asked if he wanted, anything Stuart wanted two hot dogs with onions and mustard. Then he told Graham to get himself something.

Graham left and Stuart said he might run off with the money "yes he might but it's a test to see what he'll do any way if he comes back we'll give him a chance. I think he has been under a lot of stress. I think he has been physically and mentally abused but we have to stick by the rules we make" fifteen minutes later, all three ate their food. Thirty minutes later rules had agreed.

Chapter 15

The car park at the golf course was not very busy and he easily spotted Graham Greenlaw's jeep. It would have been easy to spot the jeep if the car park was busy, it was a large black jeep with dark tinted windows the wheels the rims were alloy and the tyres were the largest he had ever seen and the chunkiest. The front grill had four huge driving spotlights that sat in front of silver bull bars. It reminded Dr Newbury of a baddie in a gangster movie. How apt he thought to himself. He deliberately parked his car [a modest little rover estate] at the other side of the car park. He got out the motor, went to the back, removed his clubs and headed to the clubhouse. There he met up with Graham; he had grown up since he first made his way to the lab twelve years ago. It had been hard for his father to get used to the fact that he had a son. A boy, which Stuart had never had wanted. He helped Graham come to terms with his past. In addition, tried to make amends for what he did to his son. Even though he had helped Stuart with coping through the rough times and there had been a change in Graham Dr Newbury still did not trust him. Today he was meeting for a round of golf because Stuart had asked him to keep an eye on him whilst he was abroad. He was helping clear the aftermath off an earthquake. He would be gone for a few months yet. This meeting with Graham convinced him that Stuart did not trust him either. Things were all right until Graham suddenly moved out of Stuarts home and he left the lab and got another job. He found one on the outskirts of the city. Working in the new forensic lab, He was still there today Both Dr Newbury and Stuart had the same feeling that he had done something and tried to find out what it was. However, to no avail.

"I checked us in and we are due to tee off in about forty-five minutes. Do you fancy a coffee"? Stuart called to the doctor as he appeared through the door.

"Yes but give me five I need to change won't be long. Make mine a latte no sugar," he answered as he headed to the changing rooms.

When he went into the lounge, Graham was sitting at the window watching some of the golfers teeing off. He went over and sat opposite him.

"Have you heard from Stuart Lately?" he asked reaching out for the cup of steaming hot liquid. He did not use the word dad or father because he knew that neither Stuart nor Graham liked the word "Only what I told you last week. He must be busy that he has not written or phoned. He reckons that he could be out there for another six weeks." He said. "How are things with you have you been keeping yourself busy".

Dr Newbury said "it's always busy in the private health care that's why I do it how's things at the forensics any thing exciting happening".

Graham paused for a moment as he considered his answer he did not want to give anything away he was not sure how the Doctor would react to what he had found out so he cleared his throat and replied "not much at the moment. It's been quiet".

The doctor read between the lines, the question he had asked seemed straight forward but the pause told him that there was something not quite right. He was about to ask Graham another question about work to see if he could figure out what he was hiding, when a steward came over to them and informed them that it was five minutes to their teeing off. Therefore, they finished the coffee and headed to the starting box.

The weather was cloudy but dry and there was a slight breeze. The doctor took a coin from his pocket and asked, "Heads or tails"

Graham chose tails and lost.

"Do you want to make it a little more exciting will we say fifty pound to the one with the lowest score" asked the Doctor.

Holding out his hand, he hoped that they could seal the deal. Graham shook as an acceptance. They played the first three holes in silence, which the doctor won two. As they walked over to the next tee, the doctor asked Graham if he could use the lodge this weekend. Graham seamed to be flustered at this request and said "It has been locked up for the last six months and I'm not sure if it was ready to be used and I was going to go up later this week and give it the once over I think the kitchen needed painted".

"I could give you a hand I didn't have anything important on and I could reschedule my morning surgery," he said as he watched the look of horror on his face.

The doctor again thought that there was something going on. Graham turned his back on the doctor as he said that he would not need a hand but he would have it ready for him the following weekend if that were any good. That certainly rattled him because he lost the next five holes. This is going to be the easiest fifty pound he was ever going to make as he gave himself a little smile as he placed his golf ball on the tee and lined his shot. The swing was perfect as he watched the ball go straight down the fairway. Graham stood at the tee with his ball waiting on him. He took a couple practice swings and then lined himself up ready to take his shot. He hit the ball all wrong and it curved of the fairway into the rough.

"Someone's having a bad day you seem a trifle stressed this morning is everything okay," the Doctor asked.

"Yes just that I had a bad night last night and I think that all this fresh air is making me tired" he replied.

"If you want we can play just nine holes and call the bets off. We can arrange it for another time". The Doctor said.

Graham seemed to be relieved that he for the moment he was of the hook. When they got back to the clubhouse, Graham went straight to his jeep and drove of at a rather high speed. This made the doctor even more determine to find out what he was doing.

Chapter 16

James was feeling better. However, James knew he could not to leave the house. There was an appointment made for him to attend the clinic later that day to have his dressings changed. It had been three days since he had came out of the clinic and he hoped that when he saw the Doctor that he would let him walk about because he was getting fed up with the wheelchair. Thanked god that he had only to use it temporary, as he could not imagine having to depend on one full time. He sat in the conservatory that looked out over the bay. He watched the boats in the harbour bobbing up and down with the waves. There were old men sitting at their huts, which sited along the side of the high wall on the pier. He knew most of them as he spent a lot of tome fishing from the pier before he got his dingy. He had even gone to sea with them in their boats. He picked up his binoculars and watched them working on their nets and lobster pots. Then he looked further out over the bay and saw a few sailing boats. There was not much wind and he could see that a few were struggling. Further, out he saw a large container ship heading towards the open sea. There he watched the world go by. Here he was stuck inside the house. The twins were at school and Jack had gone for a meeting with the accountant.

Mary had popped out to the supermarket to get a few messages. He put the binoculars down and wheeled himself to the kitchen. He was order not to touch the cooker or anything that could result in him hurting himself. He looked around and decided that it could not do any harm to make a coffee. He put the kettle on and gathered the rest of the things he needed. He did not want to reach to high to where the mugs were so he looked in the dishwasher there were mugs the dishwasher but as it had not been switched on they were still dirty. He decided that it would take too long to use the washer so he took one out and wheeled over to the sink. He was not able to reach the taps so he put the break on and pulled himself up using the bunker. He was very unsteady and his legs tired very quickly. He had just washed the mug when he heard the front door opening and heard Mary.

"In the kitchen" he shouted, "just about to make a coffee would you like one?" He offered.

Mary appeared at the kitchen door laden with carrier bags.

"I'll get that don't want you burning yourself," she said as she entered the kitchen.

"I'll get it and you can supervise," he said.

Mary could see that he wanted to get the coffee so she said

"Okay" but watched very carefully.

Once he made the coffee, Mary carried them to the kitchen table. Then went into one of the bags and brought out a cream cake. "I bought this especially for you. Hope that you will not be telling the others. That I'm spoiling you". She said and tried to put a stern look on her face but that just made James laugh.

"Is Jack taking us to the clinic or will we need a taxi," James asked between mouthfuls of cake.

"He said that he would try to get back from the accountants in time to take us. But it depends how long the accountant will take" she said wiping bits of cream from James's face much to his annoyance.

"Is the business in trouble?" he said sounding a bit concerned.

"Not according to Jack he thinks that everything going well. And it was Jack that made the appointment to see him not the other way" she said.

"Wonder what he wants to see the accountant for" James asked,

"Not sure he didn't really say and I never asked as it hasn't got anything to do with me" she replied.

She did know because Jack had asked her advice and she that told him to speak to the accountant. Jack had asked her not to tell James the reason why he was at the accountant. If he did not ring her she was to get a taxi to the clinic and he would try to be backing home when they got back.

"Are you ready to go to the clinic; it looks like we will need a taxi. I'll phone for one". Mary said as she helped James put on his jacket.

Five minutes later the driver was helping James into his taxi and Mary was folding the wheelchair so that the driver could put it in the boot. Once they were on there way James said, "Do you think that the doctor will let me use crutches, because I really hate that wheelchair. If I promise to rest do you think he will trust me and let me leave the chair with him?"

"We will just have to wait and see he won't have you using the wheelchair if you don't need it. So do not pester him. He knows what he is doing trust him".

Mary said hopping that he would be able to use crutches she knew how hard it must be for him to be immobilised. He was always doing something and was rarely still.

Chapter 17

When they got into the clinic, the nurse took them to a room down the corridor. The same nurse attended to him when he came into the clinic after the accident. This was a relief to him, as he knew whom she was

"Well James how are we feeling? The nurse asked him.

"I'm feeling alright but" he hesitated and looked at Mary from the corner of his eye. Then said, "It's my legs they feel very weak. When I to stand earlier they were shaking like jelly".

He saw Mary's face then he added, "I only stood long enough to wash out a mug. Nothing happened and I sat down when they started to shake.

Mary said, "what if you had fallen there was no one to help you. I told you that I would be ten minutes. I thought that you had everything that you needed until I got back"

The nurse saw that Mary was beginning to be worked up and she said, "Boys will be boys trying to think that they know best but thankfully there is no harm done"

This brought some comfort to Mary. Then James who now realised that he had upset Mary bowed his head and mumbled "sorry".

The nurse came forward to help James on to the couch. Then said "Don't go getting upset the pair of you we all make mistakes that's how we learn there's no-one perfect. And" she looked at Mary and told her "you do a magnificent job.

Now let's have a look at this war wound soldier"

When she had carefully removed the dressing, she gave a smile and said, "The wound looks clean there's no sign of any infection. I am just going to call Doctor Newbury and let him have a look".

She went over to the phone and spoke to the Doctor. James looked across at Mary who was sitting on a chair opposite she was aware that he was looking at her so she lifted her head, smiled, and mouthed the words its okay. James returned the gesture with a huge smile then said, "Look at the wound it's starting to heal".

Mary got up and went across to have a look and to give the lad a hug. She looked down at the wound in his leg and could see that it was starting to heal. She was pleased that the leg was looking a lot better than it did a few days ago. She let her mind wander back to the night that James was lying here in this clinic hallucinating, having a bad time, and getting everyone worried. The noise of the door opening brought her back. She gave a small shudder. Doctor Newbury washed his hands in the sink that was in the corner. Mary watched him ever since she had been a child she was mesmerized the way doctors washed their hands.

She started washing her hands the same way. She loved the way they felt clean. When he came over to the couch Mary stood back to let him in beside James. He looked at James's leg and said, "Well you seem to be healing rather quickly everything looks great. How does the leg feel?" he said looking at James.

James frowned and gave a quick glance at Mary. Who raised her eyebrow as if to say its okay you can tell him I will not get annoyed this time. He looked at the doctor and told him that he had tried to stand on his own and his legs felt wobbly.

"Well now we will have to get them to stop wobbling won't we." He smiled at James. "I think we should send you to the physiotherapist can't take you up on the offer to go fishing if I have to carry you now can we". He said to a smiling James.

With that, he turned to the nurse and asked her to phone the physiotherapist and ask her to come along and see James. Then turned to James checked the wound once more and then told him to keep up the good work and we will be out fishing in no time. He then put a new fresh dressing over the wound. This time he didn't put any bandages on he put a thing on like a giant Elastoplasts and said "this will do until you have seen the physiotherapist then we will see how the leg holds up to some movement. Perhaps we won't have to heavily bandage it". He said walking to the door. "See you in about thirty minutes". Then he was gone.

The door opened and a middle-aged woman wearing a tracksuit and her hair tied back came through the door smiling and came to the couch where James had been lying.

He sat up when she came into the room and greeted her with a smile.

"Well James" she said looking through a folder that she produced from under her armpit

"The doctor wants me to give you a few exercises to see if your leg will not burst open with movement. We don't want to open the wound now do we?" she said.

James looked at her then just nodded then he looked over to Mary who gave him a reassuring smile.

The physiotherapist looked at the wound, sucked air through her lips, and said, "That looks a sore one want to tell me how it happened".

James panicked for a second this was the first time he could remember anyone asking what happened. He could not tell them the truth. He couldn't tell them that he was running around like a deer after eating some raw meat from a slaughtered deer on the moor and how he tried to leap over the fence that was between the woods and the moor {which ironically was there to keep the wild deer out}. Staring at the wound he kept his head down then said, "I fell from a fence that I was trying to climb", and then prayed that she did not ask any more questions about it.

Luckily she did not she said "fences weren't supposed to be climbed that's why there are gates" and then she started to work on his leg.

She lifted it pulled it turned and pushed it. Sometimes it was sore and he would gasp and grit his teeth. However, not all the time he was staring at the wound praying that wound would split and that it held out till the physiotherapist was finished. Twenty-five minutes later, she finally laid lids leg down and put the pad back in place. Just as she finished there was a knock on the door and the doctor came in.

"How did this young soldier do then" he asked the physiotherapist.

She smiled and replied, "He'll live to fight another day his wound has withstood all my manhandling and looks well"

James smiled when he heard this and hoped that he would be able to go home without the wheelchair.

When the physiotherapist had, left Doctor Newbury brought a chair over to the couch where he placed it in front of James with the back facing James and sat down. The way the cops sat down in the police program that James watched on the television every Saturday morning before he went to the coffee shop. Leaning over the back, he stared at James for a moment. He cleared his throat and said, "Your leg has still a long way to go before it's healed properly so we have to be really careful. As we don't want to make the wound open up or we might have to give you more surgery and that's the last thing we want"

He looked across at Mary who seemed to be taking in everything that he was saying and was nodding as he spoke...

He then turned to James and said, "If I was to let you home with a set of crutches will you promise to rest and do the exercises that the physio gave you and no heroics or you will be back in the wheelchair." He looked straight at James who was nodding furiously so much that he told James that if he didn't watch his head was going to fall off.

James was smiling from ear to ear as he promised that he would behave himself and no heroics.

The doctor said "I think that we should put on a heavy dressing as I am afraid that James might accidentally knock or bump his leg and injure himself more and if you can get him this" he said to the nurse as he handed her a prescription.

"I'm going to give you some painkillers as I think James might be sore tonight as he has had a lot of physiotherapy Mary" he said as he walked over to a cupboard and brought out a pile of bandages and placed them on a tray.

He then put on a pair of surgical gloves and then went over to James. James watched the doctor as he put on a new dressing and bandages on his leg. When he was finished, he asked James if he thought any more about their fishing trip.

"No I was going to wait until I got better before I did anything".

"Maybe it will give you something to do. Making sure that you have everything ready I might even drop my rods and things off and you can make sure everything is in good working order". Doctor Newbury said as he worked on James's leg.

James smiled and said "good idea you can bring your things over tonight and I'm sure Mary will make dinner for you". They both looked at Mary who was standing open mouthed.

They both laughed and Mary said "yes. Dinner will be about seven hope you like chilli".

There was a knock on the door, the Doctor said in his professional voice "come in" the door opened, and the physiotherapist came in with a set of crutches and helped James become used to them. Twenty minutes later Mary and James were getting into a taxi and heading home.

Chapter 18

James was very chatty on the way home and asked Mary if she knew why Jack had not appeared at the clinic to pick them up. Mary wanted to tell him but she knew the reason why, she was excited herself, and could not wait to get home to see James's face. The taxi seemed to take forever to reach their house.

There was no-one home when the taxi pulled into the drive. This disappointed Mary she had hoped that Jack would be at home. She really wanted to see James's face but now she would have to wait. Instead, she helped James out of the taxi and into the house; he wanted to be in the kitchen with Mary to help prepare the chilli for tonight's dinner.

"Can I make some garlic bread and I could make one with cheese on it as well?" he asked Mary who had her head in the fridge

"Yes that sounds good. I am just going to phone the Hutts to send the twins back home and I need to ask them to get some cheese and milk as I forgot to get it this morning. Give me a minute and I'll put the kettle on and make us a cuppa," She said.

James asked if he could make the cuppa whilst she phoned. Mary agreed to this and watched James out the corner of her eye as she busied herself to make it less obvious that she was keeping an eye on him. When he had put the kettle on to boil she went to the hall to phone the twins to come home and get a few things from the shop. She checked her watch it was nearly five and there was still no sigh of Jack. She let out a sigh as she walked through to the kitchen and subconsciously said "oh dear I hope he's alright?"

"Course I'm all right I was only making a coffee James said as he thought it was him she was referring to

"No no not you it's your brother I thought he would have been home before now.

I hope that everything went okay at the accountants. He hasn't phoned yet." She said sounding a bit concerned.

"Maybe he has had to go to the shops to deal with something" James replied trying to ease Mary's mind "he'll come back when it's time to eat you know how much he likes your chilli". He added.

The sound of the door opening made them both turn around. It was Mr Thom, the gardener with a basket of freshly picked vegetables. Mary could use some soft fruit as dessert. He asked James how he was feeling and how the leg was healing. He said goodbye to them and left. James thought that Mr Thom was a rather weird person he hardly spoke and only came into the house to hand the fruit and veggies in James had tried to speak to him on many occasions but he had only ever answered with one-word answers. In the end, he had given up and only waved or greeted him with a hello or bye.

The twins came in to the kitchen all chattering and swinging a bag with the shopping that Mary had asked them to get.

"What's for dinner?" Sarah asked

"I'm starving" Emma chipped in.

"Chilli and you need to go and get washed and changed we are having a guest and I would like you to be clean and well behaved" Mary instructed trying to usher the two of them up stairs.

"Who is it?" Emma asked.

"It's Doctor Newbury James invited him he's bringing his fishing gear over to let James get it ready for a fishing trip they are planning" Mary informed them

"Ooh did you hear that Emma your boyfriend is coming to dinner will you sit next to him" teased Sarah.

Emma went bright red, yelled, "He's not my boyfriend I only said I liked him", and pushed a giggling Sarah out of the way.

"Don't you be saying that tonight and upsetting Emma and embarrassing everyone?" Mary said sternly to Sarah.

"Now get yourself ready. Then come down and help set the table," Mary said as she left them to sort themselves out and headed to back the kitchen.

Things were on schedule in the kitchen when the front door opened and Jack came in. He looked like he had won the lottery. He came into the kitchen where Mary the twins and James was sitting. Mary looked at Jack and knew by the smile that he had the surprise for James. He went over to James and said, "got something to show you, come with me" and helped James to his feet.

Then helped him to the front door where he stopped "stand there" he said as he positioned James right in front of the door.

"Now close your eyes and no peeping" Jack ordered his brother.

He was a bit sure what to do or say? He knew that Mary would not let Jack do anything to hurt him so he quietly went with it. He closed his eyes as instructed he could here the twins giggling behind him and he felt Mary's hand on his shoulder this small act gave him some comfort, as he still did not trust Jack. He heard the door click from the front door and could feel the cool breeze as the door opened.

"Now keep your eyes closed and I'm going to help you take two or three steps out side but remember to keep your eyes closed tightly,"

Mary said as she ushered him towards the door.

James could hear the twins oohing and aahing and wondered what it could be. He stood there wanting to open his eyes but fear that his brother might snap. He decided it would be better to wait until Jack told him to open his eyes. It was not long before Jack told him to open his eyes. He just stood and stared he was totally speechless. There before him stood a brand new yacht.

It had a white body there was a double dark blue line that went the full length of the yacht

"It has a kitchen and a bed" Emma squealed

"Look there's a toilet to and there's another bed in here," shouted Sarah as the two looked around the yacht.

Jack led James to the rear of the yacht

"Look there is a twin engine so that it can go a lot faster than your old one," Jack said as he handed the keys over to James.

Who still found it hard believe what he was seeing and now what he was hearing. Mary came round to the back of the yacht to where the boys were standing and put her arms round the two of them and said "it's nice to see you both smiling.

This is a nice yacht. You will have to get someone to show you how to use it properly. We do not want any more accidents. The noise of a car coming up the drive brought all the chatter, the giggles from the twins to a halt the car parked near to where they were all standing and the door opened, and the Doctor got out

"Well well look what we have here. That is a fine yacht you have there. Where did it come from?" asked the doctor.

James found his tongue and said, "Jack brought it home with him tonight and he has given me the keys so that means that if I have the keys it must be mine"

He held the keys up and that is when he saw the key ring it was a leather fob with his name on it. He could feel the tears' welling up it was his really his yacht he could feel his head swimming this was all too much he had to steady himself. Mary saw this and went over to hold him up. "

I think we had better go in and make sure the dinner is not burning that would be the last thing we need all these hungry mouths and no food. Come on we can come out after dinner" they all headed indoors.

The table was set in the dinning room, which looked out to the front, and James picked a seat where he could keep an eye on his yacht. The three men sat at the table. Mary and the twins helped to bring the starter through.

"Hope you like melon I can get you something else if you don't like it" Mary said as she came through the door carrying a large tray with the starters on it the twins followed each carrying small plates with crackers on them.

"No melon will be fine don't worry" the Doctor answered as he stood up to help Mary with the tray.

Everyone sat down and tucked in to the melon there was not much talking, as everyone seemed to be hungry. When the next course was brought through and James announced, "I made the garlic and the garlic and cheese breads I hope you like garlic because I used loads"? James said feeling rather proud that he had helped with the meal even though it was a small part.

"I love garlic used to eat it raw," replied the Doctor.

Emma and Sarah both screwed their face up at the thought of eating raw garlic. The main course went down well and the conversation picked up the all chatted quite comfortably with each other. Everyone seamed to be relaxing, the evening was going well, and everyone had started to play charades. As the Doctor stood up to take his turn there were bright light from a car coming up the drive way that shone straight into the dinning room. Mary and Jack both stood up and went over to the window.

"That's strange we weren't expecting anyone. Not this late". Mary said.

"It's the police," Jack said as he started to go towards the door.

The Doctor saw the look of fear on the twins and James's faces. He went over to them and put his arms around them.

"Its bad news I know it" James said his voice was almost breaking.

The doctor tightened his arm around him to let him know that he was here and everything was going to be ok.

Chapter 19

The detective followed Mary into the dinning room where he saw the doctor and he looked slightly relieved that the doctor was here to help support the children, as the news that he had was not good. He cleared his throat and was about to speak when Emma screamed "No its bad isn't it"?

The detective looked at Doctor Newbury as if he needed his permission to speak. He cleared his throat again and asked if he could have a word with him. Both men went into the hall where the detective told the doctor "they have found a body and it's believed to be that of Julian Costello, but we need someone to identify the body it's a mess.

"Two hikers come across the body and called us. The body, which appeared to left in the middle of nowhere but forensics, reckon that he was killed elsewhere. There was no sign of Andrea but who ever did this is a monster. Glad you were here I wouldn't want those kids to see their father in the state he was in perhaps you could come to the mortuary and identify the body"

"Oh my god" replied the doctor.

He continued, "We need to let the family know what is going on. I will speak with them and meet you in your car".

The detective left the house as the doctor entered the dinning room. He saw the twin's tearstained faces and their slight bodies shaking. Mary was comforting them the best she could and she was trying to hold back the tears. Jack who had his back to him was staring out the window. He to be crying to his breathing was heavy and erratic his shoulders were jerking up and down every moment or so he would lift his head up and look to the ceiling as if he was asking god why?He looked at James he was sitting inthe chair with his head buried in to a pillow he to be sobbing uncontrollably. He looked at Mary and shook his head.

He closed the door and said, "They have found a body".

This brought more sobbing from the twins who were close to hysterical. He continued, "They need to identify the body to find out if it's your father".

Jack swung round his face red and tearstained and said, "Do you want me to identify the body? I don't know if I can I've never seen a dead body".

The doctor was quick to reply, "I can do it if you want after there won't be a problem as I'm your family doctor and also a friend of the family. I would be more than happy to identify the body. Mary I will come right back and help out if the worst scenario happens".

Mary could only nod her head. She could not trust herself to attempt to speak, as she knew she had to be strong. She had known the family for nearly fourteen years and she was feeling as much pain as the children but she could not let them see her upset. The doctor bowed his head and headed for the door.

He sat in the police car as the detective headed to the morgue.

"Do you know the family?" he asked the detective.

There was a long pause before the detective answered.

"They are an influential family most people know who they are. I personally know off them but I have not met them".

The doctor let out a sigh he had hoped that this man knew the family then he could say wither it was of Julian Costello. The detective radioed the station to let them know that he had been to the Costello's house and that he had the doctor with him who had agreed to come and identify the body.

"Can you tell me anything about the circumstances that the body was found"?

The detective glanced over to the doctor and replied "More than my jobs worth".

The doctor decided that he was not going to get any information so he sat for the rest of the journey in silence.

The police car pulled into the car park of the City forensic and pathology lab. He drove the car round the back of the building. As they drove passed the main car park he scanned the area to see if Graham's jeep was there. He was relieved to see that it was not, as he was the last person that he wanted to see. There was something very strange about Graham that the Doctor did not like. What made it worse was that he did not know why, or what it was. The car stopped and two plain clothed officers met them and led them into the morgue the two plain clothed officers took him into a side room and produced some paper work that he had to read and sign. Then they took him through the procedure and when he felt ready, they led him through a door that had a large sign saying authorized persons only beyond this point.

He walked into the autopsy lab. Everything was stainless steel and the walls were white tiles then he noticed the trolley in the centre of the room. There was a white sheet covering the body. He could clearly see the out line of a body beneath the sheet he could make out the head and he looked like the same build as Julian. For the first time in his life, he felt physically sick. He had dealt with many bodies in his time and he was never put up nor down was he actually dreading that moment he wanted to walk back out the door but the thought of Jack having to come and identify this body made him stay. Any way it might not even be Julian. A man wearing a green gown, the same kind that the surgeons wear in the operating theatres was waiting at the head of the body. He stayed there until the doctor went over to the trolley and nodded to him to remove the sheet to let him see the face. The doctor looked down at the white pristinely clean sheet that covered the body that lay before him. He tried to imagine the state of the body. He closed his eyes and nodded to the man in the greens. He heard the rustle as the sheet was removed he waited for a few seconds before he opened his eyes. At first, he could not tell if the body belonged to that of Julian. His face swollen so badly that it was unrecognisable it looked like it was going to burst. There was also much of what looked like bruising. He blinked two or three times. That seemed to help his eyes focus more. He was about eighty percent the body was that of Julian's.

"can I see the rest please I need to check some scars that he had" he asked, his voice shaking the man in the greens looked over to the detective who stood at the table close to the door that they had came through earlier. He came over to the trolley, put his hand on the doctor's shoulder, and said in a soft voice "sir the remains of the body are really bad I know that you are used to seeing corpses. But when it comes to a close friend it's a whole different ball game"

"I can't be one hundred percent sure that it is Julian.' I did a ligament operation last year on his left leg and I had to remove a lump two inches above his patella. If you can let me see the left leg around that area please," asked the doctor never lifting his head. The detective nodded to the man. The doctor heard the sheet rustling as the man prepared the left leg so that the doctor could examine it. When Doctor Newbury saw the leg, he knew that the body lying on the cold stainless steel trolley was that of Julian Costello. He gave a sharp intake of air through his nostrils to help with the shock that is when he smelt the stench of rotten flesh this made him feel queasy, and he reached into his pocket to get his handkerchief. He turned to try to make an escape and bumped right into the detective who was standing behind him. The detective ushered him to the table while the man in greens removed the trolley. The detective went into a drawer, pulled out a bottle of whiskey, poured a large one, handed it to the doctor, and ordered him to down it. Doctor Newbury did as the detective had ordered. When he finished the detective poured another one for him and one for himself.

"We need to talk come with me to my office, it's just along the corridor" said the detective as he walked towards the door followed by the doctor.

The detective's office was small with books from floor to ceiling... The floor had a carpet, with a steel grey short pile, which you could just see, as there were piles of folders strewn around. His desk took up a lot of space and it faced the door. It was an old fashion desk, it reminded him of the one his father used in his office that he had in one of the rooms in their large country house. There was a folder lying open on the desk. The detective pulled a chair over so the doctor could sit at the desk he sat at the other side and pushed the open folder to the doctor.

"Appreciate if you would read this". The doctor looked at the detective and raised an eyebrow

"Isn't it confidential"?

The detective looked him in the eye and replied "we need all the help we can get on this one there was no clues. Even when the Costello has vanished, there was nothing; their bank accounts have been untouched. Their credit cards had never used since their disappearance. There was not even a ransom note. When their car had been located, we still could not get anything on it, clean we cannot even find the person whom tipped us off about it. The whole thing leads to dead ends. We are getting nowhere fast on this one. We need to know if you knew of any feud between Mr and Mrs Costello. Could Mrs Costello have paid to have her husband killed"?

Doctor Newbury head was spinning he knew that the Costello's marriage was over a long time ago, but they were amicable and although they both lead separate lives they both cared for the family and each other. They would never do anything to hurt each other.

"No. they really cared for each other. I could not believe for one minute that either of them would hurt each other. Or get a contract killing ordered on the other one".

The detective was flicking through some papers that he took out of a buff coloured folder that had Julian Costello written on the front in large red letters. The folder didn't look like it had much in it and Doctor Newbury wondered if the only sheets of paper the detective had in his hands were the only papers that were in the file. The detective looked up and said, "now that the body has been identified the forensic boys will start on the body and see if they can shed any light on this case".

He noted the shift in the Doctors position and the uneasy look that came across his face and he wondered how much he was hiding. He continued to stare at the doctor as if he was waiting for him to speak.

Doctor Newbury noticed this and said, "I know nothing of the death or murder and the disappearance of the Costello's. I have known them on both personal and professional acquaintances for a long time and there is no way I have anything to do with this" he said trying to keep control of his temper, with his hands waving at the folder that lay on the detective's desk. He looked at the detective and met his eyes and for a moment, both men locked in each other's gaze. The detective was first to look away. For a split moment, he believed that he was innocent. The detective stood up and asked if he wanted a lift home.

"Yes please if you would be so kind" a touch of sarcasm in his voice, told the detective that he had rattled the cage.

"But I'll be staying at the Costello's but if the driver can stop at my place so that I may pick up a few things first" he added.

"Bloody taxi service," the detective said as he walked towards the door, then he hesitated and said "I'll take you, come on" and disappeared through the door.

Great the last thing that I want is to be in this detective's company any longer than I have to, the Doctor thought.

As the detective drove his car through the car park, Doctor Newbury noticed Graham's jeep in the car park, and graham running towards it. Seem to be in a hurry for some reason and wonder what.

Chapter 20

He sat in silence looking out of the side window for most of the journey lost in his thoughts who did this and why. The Costello's were a law-abiding family. The people in the village respected them. The family had roots in the village for three generations and it was in the village that their business was first set up before opening a larger coffee shop in the town. They had also set up local traders committee, which was still up and running to this date. Who would do such a terrible thing to them and, he let out a heavy sigh it had only occurred to him that Andrea was still missing. He took a deep breath and rubbed his hands up and down his face breathing heavily. The detective looked at him "you okay" he said sounded a bit concerned.

"Can you stop the car I think I'm going to be sick" he managed to say in between gasps of air.

This head was swimming he felt like the one he was going to pass out. He fumbled with the door handle trying to escape the confines of the car. The detective reached passed him and released the handle the door sprung open and Doctor Newbury almost fell out of the car. He stumbled to the rear of the car where he threw up. The detective got out of the car and came round to where the doctor was. The doctor had both his hands on the boot of the car. His head hung low between his arms, his legs were apart and the detective could see them shake.

"You going to be alright or do I need to call for help because you don't look to good" asked the detective.

"Just give me a minute I'll be fine. It has just occurred to me that you have only Julian's body. Andrea is still missing or her body has not been found yet and I have to tell the kids that".

The doctor said beginning to compose himself

"I could radio for a couple of uniforms to go ahead and tell them if you want?"

He straightened himself up and said, "No I think it will be better if it came from someone they know". He took a deep breath and said to the detective "let's go".

They both got into the car and headed towards the doctors house.

The car parked in the doctor's driveway both the men got out and headed to the front door. Doctor Newbury looked over his shoulder to see the detective follow at his heels. When he had unlocked the door he stood back and let the detective enter his house first. He will take a good look round but I have nothing to hide. He thought to himself as the detective passed him and entered the house.

"Kitchen's through there if you want to make a coffee. I take two sugars and milk. I won't be long just need to get a few things," Doctor Newbury shouted sarcastically as he went into his bedroom.

He put some clothes, a towel and his toilet bag into a suitcase. Then he checked the windows, put the light out, closed the door and went to look for the detective. He found him in the study looking at the papers on his desk. He put them down when he heard the Doctor come into the study.

"Continue I have nothing to hide you are welcome to search all you want" the Doctor said as he walked towards the detective.

"Sorry it's a habit. You know what they say a detective is never of duty".

"That's not good for your health you need to step back sometimes," commented the doctor.

The detective pointed to the book shelve "there's your coffee. You're out of milk used the last in these". He said lifting a mug of coffee to his lips.

"Cheers" said the doctor. "Where did you find Julian's body? Was it close to where their car washad been found?

"Too early to say we will know more when the forensic boys are finished" he finished his coffee headed to the kitchen and the doctor followed.

"We need to get you to the Costello's they've waited long enough. He said walking towards the door.

The doctor asked the detective be dropping him at the bottom of the drive. He opened the car. He felt the cold night air hit him as he got out of the car. He opened the back door pulled out his suitcase

"Please keep me informed," he asked the detective.

"Oh we will don't worry. Don't you be taking of now?" the detective answered.

The doctor watched him drive off into the night and wondered if the detective thought that he was a suspect. He turned and started to walk up the drive. He was dreading having to tell the kids about their father. The house was lit up. Most of the lights in the front of the house were on. He thought it made the house look warn and inviting, unlike the news he was about to tell them.

Chapter 21

He slowed down as he approached the front door. This was going to be the hardest thing that he had ever had to do. He stood in the shadows watching the twins playing in one of the front rooms they looked a bit happier than they did when he left with the detective earlier. He saw Mary enter the room carrying a tray and the twins were joined by James and Jack they all sat round the table and ate what he thought would be their supper. He decided to wait until they had all finished, then go in, and tell them the devastating news.

It was about thirty minutes later when he went up to the door and entered the house. The first person he met was Mary. She took one look at him and knew that it was bad news. He looked at her but did not say anything. She went into the kitchen he followed and made him a strong cup of tea and poured him a whisky. He downed the whisky then picked up the cup and headed to the front room where everyone was waiting. When he opened the door, he felt the atmosphere change from a happy one to one of fear and uncertain.

He looked at each of their innocent faces and he felt his heart snap. He was about to speak when Jack beat him to it.

"How many bodies did they find?"

"One only one".

The twins were sitting together, he saw them reach out to each other, and he saw them entwine their fingers around each other and shuffle closer. He saw James with his head bowed so low that his head almost touched his knees. He looked at Jack the head of the family now. Himself only just a teenager he should not have this worry on his shoulders. He met his eyes they were blank. Waiting to hear what he already knew. He just did not know if it was his father or mother.

"Doctor Newbury please can tell us who it was," pleaded Jack.

"It was your father" he replied the twins both screamed and hugged each other Mary went over to them and put her arms around and tried to comfort them. James had doubled and was sobbing uncontrollably into a cushion. Jack had turned towards the window. He had his hands over his face and his shoulders were shaking indicating that he too was crying. He went over to Jack and put his hand on his shoulder.

"I'm here to help anything you need I'll be here. It is the least I can do your father and mother have been friends for many years."

Jack nodded and asked if he could see his dad.

"He's in a bit of a state. I do not think the police will let you see your father now at the moment. Forensics need to do tests to see if they can get any clues about his death or who killed him. But I will see once they are finished okay" Doctor Newbury said softly to Jack.

He did not want any of the younger ones to hear what he was saying. Jack nodded. Wiping the tears from his face he said, "I need to make a phone call will you keep an eye on them," pointing to the twins and James.

"Yes don't worry I'm going to stay for a while if that's okay with you" again Jack nodded.

As he turned to leave the room, he looked at the twins huddled tightly together and his heart crumbled. They had done well getting over the disappearance of their parents and now he feared that they would be back at square one. He walked over towards them but stopped at James knelt down beside him and put his arms around his neck to comfort him. James flinched when his brother tried to comfort him and pulled away. Jack stood up and looked at the doctor, who frowned and lifted his hand to indicate to Jack to leave him for the moment. Jack walked over to the twins, got on his knees, and held them tight. He buried his face between them and spoke softly to them. After a few moments, he stood up to leave and make the phone call he said he was going to make. Both twins grabbed hold of him and started to scream. He got down on his knees and told them that he was not going anywhere he just needed to make a phone call

"I'll just be in the hall. I'll leave the door open I just want to speak to Bethany" he stroked their hair and said, "I won't leave you. I promise" he stood up and this time they let him leave the room, but watched his every move. James sat alone, still doubled over the cushion crying hysterically. The doctor went over and softly called his name. James either never heard or he ignored the doctor. Then the doctor knelt down beside James and put his hand on his shoulder and said "James I'm so sorry if there is anything you need I'm here if you want to talk I'll listen".

He kept his hand on James's shoulder and slowly James lifted his head of the pillow and looked at him then said, "What has happened to our mum? Is she dead to lying waiting somewhere? Does she know that he is dead? Because I knew that, they were. When the never came back I knew that something bad had happened. Now I can't say sorry".

Doctor rubbed James's shoulder and said, "You thought that something bad had happened to them because you knew that they would never leave you no matter what. It is only natural. It is okay. No one knows anything about your mum. All we can do now is hope and pray that she will be safe and well and be home soon. He then asked how his leg was did he need any pain relief (he chose to use the word relief rather than painkillers).

"I'm going to make a strong cup of tea for everyone," Mary said.

He looked across to Mary who was comforting the twins. "You wait here and I'll get the tea"

He walked to the door and met Jack entering the room. He put his arm on Jacks and asked, "Do you want a cup of tea or something stronger"

"Something stronger please" Jack replied.

"Come with me to the kitchen. You can help with the tea. Mary can look after the young ones," he said ushering Jack out the door.

"I'm sorry about your dad and there is anything I can do please ask". He said handing a good drop of whisky to Jack who drank about half.

Then he looked into the glass as if he was looking for answers.

"I'm a bit concerned about the twins. I hope that this unfortunate happening does not put them back. We need to get them to talk about your parents you know the good times. I do not think they will talk to me so if you or James can try it might help them come to accept what has happened. It wouldn't be good for them to go back to how they were when the news of the disappearance of your parents".

Jack listened to what the doctor was saying and agreed.

"When they have had this tea I'll take them to their bed and see if they will say anything," Jack said as he helped the doctor make the tea.

"I'll ask Mary to make the guest bedroom up for you. On one has used it since Sally was here at Christmas. However, Mary cleans it. So there will not be much needed done to it to make it comfortable. The doctor admired Jack for the way he was handling the situation. He had to do a lot of growing up this few months. They carried the tea to the front room. Poured the five mugs of hot brown liquid and passed them round.

Mary was more than pleased to go and make the guest bedroom up for the doctor. She was glad to be on her own for a few moments to grieve for one off her best friends. She was changing the bedding when she heard a soft tap on the door. "

Come in" she shouted

The door opened and the doctor popped his head round the door and asked, "Are you all right".

"Yes I was a bit relieved to come up here and sort the room for you. It has given me time to grieve. I did not want to do it in front of the children. However, I am okay now. Maybe not when they have all gone to sleep and the house is quiet,"

She said keeping her self-moving, as she was unsure if she would start to cry if she did not keep her mind busy.

"If you need anything to help you sleep let me know" the doctor said.

"Yes thanks" she said as she disappeared behind the duvet as it she flung it up into the air to help straighten the cover.

The doctor left the room and headed to the front room. Jack was just getting the twins ready to head up for their beds. The doctor noticed the way that they clung tight to Jack, but kept looking at James, who had barely moved since he nodded to him. When Jack and the twins had left, the doctor asked James if he was okay.

James replied, "All I see is my father frowning at me. That was the last thing he ever did to me was frown. Every time I close my eyes he is there frowning at me. I am feeling very tired and would like to go to my bed. But I'm scared that he'll still be there when I close my eyes".

"I can give you something that might help you sleep".

"No I will be alright when I'm in my room. He never came in there it was my escape route hopefully he won't be there tonight".

Well if he is and you have trouble sleeping just give me a shout I'm a light sleeper". James looked at him and gave a small crocked smile.

"Do you need a hand getting up the stairs? He asked James.

"No, I would like to try to do it myself. Thanks anyway".

! Okay I will compromise I will give you ten minutes and then I will bring you up some hot chocolate. Deal" said the doctor as he held his hand up for a high five.

James responded and at the same time as his hand slapped the doctor's the said "deal" and made his way slowly to the stairs as the doctor made his way to the kitchen to make three mugs of hot chocolate.

He was almost done when Jack walked into the kitchen "great minds think alike I was going to make some. Does James have to his bedroom yet? He headed that way but if you did not find him struggling up the stairs he must have made it to his room safely. How are Sarah and Emma?"

Jack gave out a heavy sigh then said "they are more concerned about the whereabouts of there mum".

"Does that upset you"? The doctor asked Jack.

"Well I think that it might not have hit them yet but then dad didn't have a lot of time for them nor James. I was his blue-eyed boy. Over the last year or so, it got worse especially for James he was always on his case about something. They had an argument just before the left. He told James that his school grades were not good and he wanted his to study harder. However, he is in the top ten in his class at most things. He's a lot cleverer than I was at school".

Why did you get him the boat then"? The doctor asked.

Jack looked over his shoulder as if to check that they were still alone.

"I managed to convince dad before they disappeared that it would be a good investment as we all could use it for holidays. Alternatively, even hire it out in the holiday season. I knew that when it was down in the harbour he would forget all about it. Therefore, that is how James got the boat. I knew how to work him so that we all got things that we really wanted. He bought me a car so I made him get a boat for James but he didn't realise that it was for James." He gave a little laugh.

"These will be getting cold," said Jack lifting two mugs of hot chocolate.

"What about the twins what will you get them"

"Oh there booked to go to Disney World with Mary in a June.

Dad did not arrange that I did earlier today that is why I could not pick them up at the clinic. It took longer than I thought". Jack answered a wee bit smugly.

"How are Sarah and Emma? Do you need me to check in on them or are you okay". The doctor enquired as he held the door open for him.

"Their both snuggled up in the same bed, but I've managed to get them talking about dad just like you said. I think they will be all right. I am going to read a story to them try to keep things as normal as I can". Replied Jack as they headed for the stairs

"Good lad" the doctor said as he ruffled the top of Jacks head. "Keep up the good work".

The doctor tapped lightly on James's door and entered his bedroom when James shouted, "it' okay you can come in"

The doctor looked around James's room there were pictures of dinosaurs on one wall. In a bookcase beside them were books and an assortment of models of every known dinosaur to man. From the roof there were mobiles made up like the universe all in the right places. Quite impressive he thought, as he looked at them moving slightly. James's bed was beside the window and as he walked over, he could see the view that James had it looked right out over the bay. The night was clear and he saw the orange glow from the lights across the water. There were a few tankers waiting on the right tide their light were all lit up their bright lights casting slithers of white across the water. Every thing outside looked so calm and peaceful unlike things in his world and he thought that things were about to get a whole lot worse. It was as if his tide was turning and turning fast, very fast.

The Doctor's mind brought back to the bedroom when James said, "my mum loved the view. Sometimes we would just sit looking out at the sea and listen to the waves. If you shut your eyes, it is almost as you are standing on the sands. When the tide is out and the wind is in the right direction, you can hear the seals on the rocks singing. My mum used to say that it was mermaids. At first, I believed her but dad spoilt when he said there are no such things as mermaids. Do you believe in mermaids"?

Doctor Newbury looked at James's hopeful expression and said, "Well just because I haven't seen any that doesn't mean they don't exist, but some one must have seen one or how else would we know what they look like. Therefore, I guess they must and therefore I do believe in mermaids". This brought a smile to the face of James.

Doctor Newbury went to James's bed and handed him the mug of hot chocolate. "How's the leg after that climb up the stair? He asked James

"It's fine. There is no pain. Just the muscle is a bit sore but that is all".James replied. He had his hands wrapped around the mug and was blowing the steam away trying to cool the contents of the mug down to a comfortable temperature to drink. The doctor plumped up James's pillows and straightened out his duvet. He switched on the nightlight that was at the side of James's bed, and watched the ceiling light up with dolphins and fish move round the ceiling as if they were in the water. James laughed

"I am not scared of the dark now. Not what I was like as a baby".

"What you mean to tell me that the nightlight is only for babies. Just look at the dolphins putting on a show for you that are beautiful. Babies only like the soft light. It is when you get older that you appreciate the beauty in the true meaning of a nightlight. Just you lie back and watch them. And soon you'll be in the show with them".

The doctor said ruffling the top of James's head. Taking the mug from him, he waited until he had settled himself down and then tucked him in. He walked towards the door, and as he turned to put the light out he could see that it would not be long before James was appearing in the dolphin show.

James drifted of to sleep as he watched the dolphins turning above his head. He saw them playing balls, balancing them on there noses, he watched them jumping through hoops, he saw them swim in crystal blue waters. He saw them jumping over him as he swam in the clear blue waters of the Indian Ocean. He swam along side the dolphins he dived deep down into the cool clear blue waters. He saw fish of all different sizes and all bright colours he swan through shoals of fish he could feel them tickle him. He watched lobsters crawl along the white sand sat the bottom of the Ocean. He loved it here; he had no worries anyone here to make him feel sad. The only thing missing was his mum.

Chapter 22

From the bed that Andrea she could see the stars. The night was clear there were no clouds, which made the temperature out side drop and because there was not any heating inside the room, she could feel the cold creep in. She shivered and tried to snuggle further under the duvet. She would have got up and walked around the room to try to keep herself warm, but the man that brought her here had tied her to the bed and she could not move. He was in the room next door cooking what smelt like chicken. The room was small and there was furnished but everything covered in dustsheets. There were no pictures on the wall. Nor could she see any books or anything to make the room homely. The place looked like it was a holiday cottage, or a place that seldom used. There was a musty damp smell about the place. It could do with a woman's touch. There was no television or radio, so Andrea recited poetry to try to keep her mind occupied. The man that brought her food and water never spoke, even when she asked where her husband was and if he was all right. She asked him everyday but he never answered. She asked him what he wanted, was it money, if so he would get whatever he wanted. She would dream about her kids the twins their innocent smiling faces she heard them laugh and giggle she saw them skipping in the garden. Then she would wake up crying as she realised it was only a dream. She prayed that they were safe and she would see them again. She dreamt of her boys playing football, Jack in goals letting James net a few. She watched them building model dinosaurs together. She heard them argue. Oh what she would do to hear them argue again. She dreamt of them all everyone except Julian she never had any dreams about him. She spent most of her day thinking about him. Where was he? She started to wonder if he had anything to do with this situation. She was startled when the door opened and the man walked in. he wore a balaclava, covering most of his face. All that was visible were his eyes. They were dark and expressionless. He must be about five foot eight. Athletic build. Andrea reckoned that he was early thirties no more than thirty-six. He always wore black overalls. His feet were always in boots and they were always polished. She tried to find out what it was like outside, she asked it there was any chance that she could have a shower or a bath as it had been a while since she had had one and she desperately needed one. The man came in one day outside the usual mealtimes, untied her hands, and pushed her through the door, along a small narrow corridor and through a door, which led to a small bathroom. The room was dirty and it looked like had not been used or a long time. There was a bath filled with hot water and looked very inviting. There were some towels, which to her surprise were clean and soft. He left but did not close the door. This disturbed Andrea a bit but she desperately needed a bath so she decided that it would have to do. She thought that if he were going to do anything to her it would have happened before now. She decided that it would be relatively safe to use the bath with the door left open. The bathroom had one small window above the cistern but there was brown paper covering it from the outside making it impossible to see outside. Andrea listened to hear if she could make out some noises. She could not hear a thing there was no noise from traffic, she could not hear any birds singing.She thought to be very strange, because if you listen you can hear a bird of some sort singing almost anywhere. Keeping her back to the door, she got her self-ready for a bath. She slowly lowered herself into the hot water and as the water covered her body, she could feel the tension ease. There was soap and shampoo sitting in the corner of the bath. She cupped one hand then massaged it into her scalp and her hair. As the smell of the shampoo surrounded her, she thought that it had a familiar smell. However, this was not the brand that she used she could not quite put her finger on where she had smelt it before. It was the same with the soap. There was a feeling in her mind that this smell was something that she knew.She put it to the back of her mind. Closing her eyes, she relaxed even more.

Chapter 23

A noise from the corridor brought her back to the present time as her eyes opened she looked over her shoulder to see what had made the noise when her eyes caught sight of a small bottle of aftershave sitting on the shelf beside the medicine cabinet. Suddenly she froze as it all clicked into place. The smell of the shampoo and of the soap, seeing the aftershave it all pointed to Doctor Newbury. Was it coincidence?

The man who had brought her food and had run her bath certainly was not Doctor Newbury. He was slightly taller and had more muscles than he had. When the man in the house left the house was he going to meet him, was he the master in this plot. Deep down her knew that Doctor Newbury would keep her and her husband captive. He had known Andrea before the birth of Carla and had been helped her cope with Carla's death. She had almost had an affair with him soon after. She only managed to stop herself from taking it further after Julian had said to her the night before she went to meet him at the library that they should try for another baby. He wanted to have a son to take over the business. He had laid the table out for a romantic meal with candles and rose petals; he even hired a top class chief. As she looked at Julian, her heart softened and she fell in love with him all over again. There was a loud knock on the door that made her jump and brought her back to the horrible bathroom and the gruffness or the mans voice made her shiver.

"Get out and dressed now," he ordered.

She waited to see if he would move away from the door. However, he did not and in an even gruffer and louder voice shouted "NOW".

She almost jumped right out of the bath. Quick as she could she grabbed a towel, wrapped it round her, and used the other one to dry herself. When she was finished, she turned around expecting him to be standing at the door. However, he was gone. She breathed a sigh of relief and headed along the corridor towards the bedroom where Andrea was living captive for the last few weeks. He appeared at the door that led into the kitchen. A startled Andrea froze to the spot waiting on him to give her the next order he wanted her to do.

This was when the stranger had first kidnapped AndreaNow she was stronger and she found out that here captor was not as strong as he was thought slowly but ever so careful she started to work him first it was little things. Saying what food she preferred to eat. Could she have a fire as she found it a little cold? This man in the black overalls met all of her requests. She began to think that if she asked for a gun he would most likely give her one. Soon she thought that using all her womanly charm she would turn the tables.

Chapter 24

A loud bang from outside woke Doctor Newbury He jumped out of bed and looked out of the window. He had almost the same view as James as the bedroom that he was in was at the front of the house, only at the other end from James's room. At first he could not see anything and was about to get back into bed when he saw movement inside James's new cabin cruiser that was sitting in the drive. Quickly he pulled on his jersey and trousers and crept down the stairs and out the front door. He crept around the outside of the boat, trying to see who was intruding in the boat. He could not see anyone but he could hear someone moving about inside. He went to the back of the boat to where there was a small boarding ladder and as quietly as a cat stalking it's prey he climbed up on to the boat and made his way to the cabin where he heard all the noise coming from. As he was about to open the door to the cabin he heard someone crying. He opened the door to find James lying face down on the bunk. James jumped when the door opened he obviously had not heard Doctor Newbury as he climbed onto the boat and made his way to the cabin.

"Are you okay" asked Doctor Newbury as he walked towards James.

James said nothing as he turned himself to face him. He just stared at the floor.

"This is one hell of a boat for a lad like you to own. You must have been overjoyed to be its owner," said the doctor as he ran his hands over they hand crafted interior of the cabin.

James sniffed, wiped his nose on his sleeve and said, "It's my entire fault I wished he was dead as they left to go to Sally's funeral. Now he is. I am to blame and when Jack finds out he will take it from me and then he will kill me. And Sarah and Emma won't have a dad any more and it's my entire fault."

Doctor Newbury looked at James's pitiful face and as he went and sat on the bunk beside him, he said, "You didn't kill him just because you wished him to die. It is not your fault how many things have you wished for that have not came true. I bet there are loads of things. Think about it. You cannot kill someone just by wishing him or her dead. You were angry with him and at the time, it is something that you did because at that time you wanted him to hurt just as if he hurt you. Believe me". He said taking hold of James's head and turning it so they were looking into each others eyes and said "it's not your fault and you never killed him" he held his gaze for a moment or two and there he saw a frightened little boy who needed his mum.

As he released the hold on him James grabbed the doctor and hugged him so tight that the doctor thought that James was never going to let go. The Doctor put his arms around James and told him that Jack need never know about what was said here in this boat tonight so don't worry because he wasn't going to hurt him again.

"Now how about I slip back into the house and grab us our duvets and pillows and we sleep in the boat. It could be fun a bit like camping but only in a boat," asked Doctor Newbury.

"Cool" replied James.

With that, the doctor got up and went to get the duvets.

The doctor did not creep into the boat this time instead he made a lot of noise and kept tripping over things. When he reached the cabin that James was in, he was laughing and said to him "I think that you have woken up the house. Perhaps he had woken up the whole street with all that noise."

The doctor straightened out James's duvet and handed him his pillows. Then made his own bed when he got comfortable, he asked James if he was looking forward to taking the boat out on the water.

"Yes I am I have to get tuition on how to handle her"

"Oh" interrupted the doctor "it's a she. What's her name?"

"I have not had time to think of one yet. But I can't wait to do her maiden voyage" James said his eyes wide with the thought of the excitement of taking his boat on the water for the first time.

"Where would you like to take her on her first trip on the seas?" he asked.

James replied without hesitation "the Indian Ocean. I want to see the blue sea because my mum said that it was the same colour of my eyes. I want to see the all the colourful fish and swim with the dolphins. Do you know if there are any sharks out there? I heard that there could be great white sharks out there".

He paused and the doctor was about to speak when he continued.

"It seams like there is always something to spoil the fun".

He thought about what James had said and tried to figure out what he meant but he heard the slow rhythm of his breathing and knew that if he asked he wouldn't tell him because James had fallen asleep to dream about is new boat and swimming in the Indian Ocean.

Mary had been up early and had a breakfast cooking. James and the doctor could smell the bacon and fried eggs as they walked through the door. Mary was surprised to see James up so early and even more surprised to see the doctor walk through the door with him.

Doctor Newbury noticed the surprised look on her face and offered an explanation. "We decided to wait until the house was asleep and then we crept out and camped out in the boat. It was fun," he said as he winked at James.

James smiled. "How did you sleep last night?" the doctor asked Mary.

"Oh I managed to keep my eyes closed after a while. However, I tossed and turned from about three o clock. Therefore, I decided to get up and keep myself occupied. So breakfasts ready if you two are". She said ushering the two campers to the table.

She poured coffee for the doctor and juice for James. Thenshe returned to the cooker to finish the cooked breakfasts off. They were eating when the letterbox rattled and Mary got up to see what the delivery had been. She returned to the kitchen with the daily papers. The doctor knew by the look on her face that the death or murder of Julian Costello was in the papers. As the paper look like it unopened, he presumed that it was front-page news.

Chapter 25

The door in the kitchen opened and a red eyed Jack walked through he looked like he had not slept. He sat down at the table and Mary brought him his usual mug of coffee, sweet with no milk. She put it down in front of him and squeezed his shoulder. He lifted his hand, placed it on top of Mary's, looked at her, and gave a crooked smile. He lowered his head and then rubbed his face the doctor knew that he was almost in tears but he seemed to be trying to hold himself together, he thought for the sake of James and the twins. James finished his breakfast then asked to if he may leave the table. When he had left Doctor Newbury made himself another coffee and sat down at the table beside Jack

"If you want I will phone the detective and asked how things are going. Then if you want I can help you with any funeral arrangements that need to be done".

He pointed to the paper and said, "It's in the papers. I have not looked at what the press have written. Do you want to read it"?

Jack did not move he just stared blankly at his table. Mary put bowl of cereal down in front of him. He pushed the cereal around the bowl but not attempted to eat anything. After about five minutes, he pushed the bowl away and drank his coffee. He had left the room without saying anything. Two or three minutes later Mary and the doctor heard the roar of Jack's car as he reversed out of the drive and sped of down the road.

"Hope he will be alright" Mary said sounding a bit concerned.

The doctor replied, "I think he just needs to be by himself at the moment. I am heading to speak to the detective that is on the case and I will keep an eye out for him. I won't be long". He got up from the table and headed for the door.

"Will you be alright? I would let the twins sleep as long as the can. See you soon. The papers might try to be in touch so keep the curtains closed and don't answer the door." he turned and went out the backdoor which Mary locked as soon as he was gone.

She went into all the ground floor rooms and closed all the curtains. Then she went up the stairs to check on James and the twins. As she passed the twins door she listened at the door to see if there was any noise coming from there room, but it was all quiet. She tapped lightly on James's door and popped her head round the door when he said for her to come in.

"Doctor Newbury has nipped out for a little while but he won't be long. He thinks we should keep the curtains closed down stairs as there might be reporters hanging about outside. We should be careful not answer the door unless we know who is calling. He has gone to see the detective and keep a look out for Jack. She said to James who was already at the window.

"That might be one of them at the gate already, there's a man waiting there and he tried to stop both Jack and the Doctor's cars. But neither of them stopped". He said as Mary joined him at the window.

"Why are they here" James asked Mary.

"Well perhaps they think they might get a story or something like that. Your father was a prominent figure in the community people want to know what has happened to him and how you are all coping. They will want to be the first to get a scoop. I think there will be more than one here soon". She said as she closed the curtains slightly.

"Makes it harder for them to get pictures if we keep the curtains closed just a wee bit. However, we do not want to shut out all the light. Any way how's the leg. Is it sore or itchy? Do you want me to ask the doctor to have a look at it when he returns? He said that he won't be too long." Mary asked as she tidied up some things in his room.

He replied, "no its feeling fine. I do not think the doctor needs to look at it. When do you think I will be able to have a proper bath I'm really missing not having one".

Mary laughed and said, "Now there's a first a young lad like you wanting to have a bath. Normally you have to be dragged kicking and screaming for one. However, I think you will have to wait until your stitches are out. I am heading down stairs is there anything other than a bath that I can get for you"

James smiled and shook his head. "I'll be down shortly just got some homework that I need to be catching up with," he said picking out some books from his backpack that he used for school.

Mary left him on his bed him reading a school book and headed for the stairs. She checked in on the twins but they were both sound asleep. Quietly she closed the door and headed down the stairs to the kitchen.

Chapter 26

Mr Thom the gardener was making himself a coffee when Mary opened the door. She jumped with fright as she saw the figure of a man there. It took her a few seconds to realise that it was only Mr Thom. He almost dropped the mug he was holding because he was not expecting anyone to come through the door at that moment.

"Seems we are all a little jumpy this morning," he said in his droll voice.

"That's bad news about the boss. How are the young ones taking it? He continued, "Young Jack passed me speeding along the road, like the devil was at his heels. Mind you, that doctor was not far behind him. He is up to no good. I would not trust him. Said all along that he was a bad apple".

Mr Thom had taken a dislike to the doctor ever since he found out about him and Andrea and made it obvious that he disapproved of the whole situation. Telling anyone who would listen to him. Things were getting out of hand and both Andrea and Julian took Mr Thom took him to one side and told him that he stops talking to everyone about what happens in their home and personnel things about their lives. Or else he would find himself out of work and in court for slander. Mr Thom stopped all the gossip and from then on hardly spoke to anyone. He came to work, did his work then went home. He only spoke to Julian and very rarely spoke to Andrea.

"Is there no word of Mrs Costello then? They just have the boss's body. Do you think that is a bit strange? You would think that if someone killed him. They would have killed her. Don't you think?" He said his droll voice grating on her making a shiver run up her spine.

She found herself thinking that if it had been Andrea's body his name would be the first that sprang to mind as a culprit. She was almost about it say something to him when he must have read her mind and announced that he would be in the greenhouse if anyone needed him. As he walked towards the door, she asked him to be vigilant as there was one reporter and she suspected there would be more. He never turned round he just mumbled and left.

Chapter 27

James looked out across the bay. The water looked so calm. There were small waves that gently rolled towards the shore some broke gently on the sandy shore. A few seagulls hovered above the small fishing boats as they prepared to head out to sea in the hope to steal a few scraps that the anglers might discard. The lifeboat was waiting on the slipway as the men that operated the station worked on her, cleaning and doing daily checks. James knew most of them and he looked over at the miniature lifeboat that they had gave him when he took all his savings from his piggy bank to them after they had been out to a major rescue. His mum had told him all about the service, and how they depended on donations from the public He had went to school, asked for donations for the lifeboat, put all his savings into a black plastic pail, and asked his mum if the coffee shop would put a collection tin on the counter. By the end of the month, his pail was almost half-full. At the weekend, he got his mum to lift the pail onto his go-kart and both of them wheeled it over to the little gift shop that was at the side of the boatshed. He watched as the woman and her assistant counted the money and told him that he had raised four hundred pounds. He felt like he was the only person in the world.

"That was a lot of money for a wee lad like you to rise," said the woman.

Two days later, there was a knock at the door. He was playing in the kitchen when his mum walked through the door with a man who was a crewperson on the lifeboat.

"This is the coxswain from the lifeboat and he was so impressed with the amount of money that you collected that he wants to reward you with a tour of the boat. Therefore, we should get our coats on and go with him to see the boat"

He will remember that day for the rest of his life when the tour was finished he got a trip out to sea on the lifeboat. He remembers waving to his mum who because she was expecting stayed at the quayside and watched her grow smaller and smaller. Then grow bigger and bigger as the headed back to the harbour. Before he came off the boat, the crew gave him a model lifeboat, which to this day he cherishes. From that day, he became hooked on boats. His eyes scanned the boat that sat in the drive and he thought I cannot wait to test her in the water but she needs a name a good name. He looked back to the sea and wished his leg were not hurt, he so wanted to be alone, alone with the fish swimming under the water with not a care about anything. He sighed looking out again he asked the world where is my mum what have you done to her, please keep her safe and let no-one harm her. His eye caught a small fluffy feather drift down from above and land on his windowsill. Gently he opened the window and picked up the feather. The feather was fluffy and very small He looked up towards the roof but there were no birds there. He smiled he knew that this feather was from his mum's guardian angel. Letting him know that the angles were keeping an eye on his mother He closed his hand around it and whispered "thank you".

He placed the feather under his pillow then went back to the window. He could see the reporter still loitering around the gate. He kept looking up the drive way and then wandering back and forward along the road. There was a police car coming along the road. The reporter had his back to it and did not see it until he turned to walk back towards the drive. When he noticed the police, he swung himself round and started to walk further away from the house. The police followed him. Then when they were close to the reporter, they put on the sirens. James laughed at the reporter as he jumped and dropped his notebook that he had been scribbling down his notes. The police officers got out of the car took his notes and ripped them up. Then the officer took some notes of his own. James could not hear what the officers were saying but it looked like the reporter was getting a ticking off he hung his head and James could see him nod every now and again. Next thing the reporter was hurrying away from the police and the house. The police car drove up the street turned at the small roundabout then parked their car. Close to the house. Near enough for comfort but far enough away go let the Costello's have some privacy.

James went to tell Mary what had happened and when he passed the twins room he could head them talking. He knocked on the door and put his head round "Hi how are you two feeling this morning? He asked them.

Emma looked at Sarah and then said "we're alright what have you been doing you look smug?"

James thought about it he was not sure whether to say anything about the papers but he knew they would find out and he thought that it would be better if it came from him so he related the story about the reporter and the police.

"Are they still parked there"? Sarah asked

"Yes. Do you want to come and see them you can see them from my room". James said as he walked to the door.

"Yes" both of them answered at the same time.

James loved the way they did that, when they both answer art the same time. He opened the door and they all trotted over to James's to watch the police from his bedroom window

James said to Emma and Sarah "I think that mum's still alive and that she is going to be alright. Look at what I found falling from the sky. I asked what has happened to our mum. This fell down and landed on the windowsill. There were no birds around" James went to his pillow, pulled the small fluffy feather out, and handed it to the twins. "You can keep it leave it under your pillow and you'll dream about her"

Sarah took the feather and went to her room where she placed the feather under her pillow. The three of them then headed down stairs to find what Mary had for their lunch.

Mary was in a large walk in pantry, she jumped when James popped his head round the door and spoke to her. She was so engrossed in in preparing their lunch that she never heard them come into the kitchen.

"You lot wash your hands and set the table I'll be there in a minute".

They placed plates and cups at the table then after their hands were washed the sat patiently waiting on Mary. She eventually appeared from the pantry carrying a tray with sandwiches and some home backing. She put the tray on the table and went to the fridge to get some of her special homemade lemonade. She was pleased to see them tuck into the food that lay before them.

Chapter 28

Doctor Newbury caught up with Jack in the viewpoint car park. It was popular with the tourists as on a clear day you could see right across the bay and watch the tankers and fishing boats as the went about there daily trips back and forth. He was sitting on one of the picnic tables looking out to the sea. The doctor bought two coffees and a couple of bacon rolls. He headed over to where he was sitting. He offered Jack a cup and one of the rolls "think you might need these since you missed breakfast" he said.

Jack took the one of the cups and one of the rolls.

Jack gave a crooked smile and then said "cheers" the two of them ate in silence the doctor asked him if he was okay.

Jack nodded but never said anything

"You had Mary a bit worried after you left in a hurry".

Jack let out a sigh then said, "I just needed to get out the house. Everything is going wrong everything is falling apart. First, my long-term girlfriend dumped me. No reason, no explanation she just phoned me she was upset but would not tell me what was wrong. She said that it is over and then she hung up. I tried to phone but it was always her mum or dad that answered I asked them to get her to call me back but she never did. I concentrated on the opening of the new shop in the hope that mum and dad would walk through the door and now dad is dead and god knows where mum is she could be alright, she could be dead, waiting to be found somewhere. I am loosing everything and I cannot stop it. Even James is drifting away from me. However, that is my own fault. He won't come near me because I beat him up once when he said that he thought that they were dead". Jack said through tears that were now rolling down his face his shoulders were shaking as he sobbed uncontrollably.

The doctor put his hand on Jacks shoulder and squeezed it gently.

Jack took a swig of coffee and continued "when the police came and told us that they had found a body and that they thought that it was dad I phoned and told Beth what was happening she wanted me to go round today I was on my way there but I needed to stop. "If you do not feel like driving over how about I take you and when you are ready to come back give me a phone and I will pick you up. But only if you let me drive your car" said the doctor to Jack.

"I've always wanted to drive a sports car". Jack went into his pocket and handed the keys over to the doctor who smiled at the thought of driving such a great motor

They both headed to the bright red sports car that was sitting in the car park near to the snack van that the doctor had bought the coffee and rolls from earlier.

The doctor sat in the driver's seat and adjusted the seat to his own comfortable position, he then familiarised himself with the gears, lights. Then when he was happy, enough he turned the ignition. As the engine roared into life he could not help the smile turning into a huge grin He put it into gear eased the car out on to the open road. Jack spoke very little on the way to his ex girlfriend parents house, the doctor thought that perhaps he was a bit apprehensive about meeting her. He only gave the doctor instructions on how to get there. When they reached the house, the front door opened and a young woman walked towards the car. She blushed when she realised that it was not Jack driving the car. It was the doctor. Her doctor, the one that she had attending for her pregnancy. She was carrying Jacks baby. She put her head down as she approached the passenger door she did not want to make eye contact with the doctor, after all, he knew all about her and her baby, which was more than Jack was knew.

The doctor watched as the two of them embraced the minute that Jack got out of the car, and as they walked up the path hand in hand, he hoped that the two of them sorted themselves out as he thought that they looked good together. He waited until they reached the front door and Jack turned round and waved to him before he drove of leaving them hugging at the door they will be fine he thought to himself as he looked at them in the rear view mirror.

Chapter 29

The doctor pulled the car into a lay-by that over looked the bay. On a clear day, you could see right across to the other side of the bay. In the distance, the dark hills rose from the grey sea like a giant wave frozen in time. When the sun shone over the top of them the looked like a large emerald jewel with a variety greens that changed depending on where the sun was. Today there was a grey mist rolling in and there was hardly any visibility. A horn blasted from the depths of the mist. Although there was a mist, the weather was still quite humid. As he sat, his mind switched to the events that had just been uncovered. He thought about Julian his body rotten, his flesh blackened and smelling terrible, he would always have that image imprinted on this mind forever. He thought about Andrea was she still alive and suffering. Had Andrea's body dumped just like that of Julian? He felt so helpless. He got out of the car as he felt the insides of his stomach rising he tried to stop but it was too late. He wretched and the content of his stomach landed on the grass verge. He took out his handkerchief and wiped his mouth, then turned it round and wiped the sweat from his brow. He put his hands on the bonnet of the car and inhaled large gulps of air. Once he had himself together, he sat back in the car. He pushed the seat back and closed his eyes.

She was there smiling and waving to him he could see her standing there the sun shining on her black hair. He loved the way that the sun lit her hair he thought it looked like an angel with her aura shining behind her he could smell her shampoo. It always had an aroma of fresh strawberries. He imagined his hands stroking her hair; his hands slid down her back and circled her ticklish spot. He could feel her wriggle as he kissed the back of her neck, she responded to his advances her soft smooth skin warmed us he stroked her neck and shoulders. His hands cupped her breasts he liked the firmness of them and a trail of butterfly kisses had her groaning with ecstasy. He could feel her hands massage his back. He felt her kisses soft and gentle yet powerful enough to send him on the road to heaven as they rained down over his tense body. He could hear her breathing as it quickened with arousal that had started deep within. He ran his hands down the curves of her slender body. He traced the out line of her soft but firm thighs. He adored the shape of her thighs not to muscle but firm. His hands worked her, she groaned with pleasure as he gently penetrated her. Soon they were lost in each other. He waited until the time was right and brought her to a climax at the same time as he climaxed. He listened to her heart beating so fast. He held her close and nuzzled her neck, he spoke her name softly she did not reply, he opened his eyes and watched her drift away. He tried to hold her but she slipped through his fingers, he called her name again only this time he spoke loud. He reached out to grasp her hand but she just smiled and then waved. She faded into the distance he shouted at her to come back but she blew him a kiss, and then was gone. The sound of a lorry as it blasted its horn rudely woke him from the dream that he had dreamt as it passed the lay-by in which stopped. He cursed It took him a few moments to realise that he had been dreaming and now he was thrown back into reality and back to all the mess. He got out of the car reached into his pocket and pulled out a cigar. As he stood there shaking slightly inhaling the cigar deeply he felt the warmth of the sun on his face. He hoped that Andrea could feel the same warmth on her face. He had stopped but now with all the events over the past few months he had started again. He did not really enjoy smoking and vowed that this would be his last packet. He started the car pulled out of the lay-by and headed to the Costello's house.

Chapter 30

Graham stared out of the window. He could not get his head round why everything had gone wrong, now he was trying to cover up a kidnap and a murder. Both of which he had never intended to happen He was trying to extort money from the Costello's after finding out about the DNA fixing that doctor Newbury had made when James had been born. He had been looking after the house when his father and the doctor had been away at a genetics conference and they had asked him to feed the doctors cat and water his plants. He had been looking through some of the books that were in Doctor Newbury's study. He opened a book written by professor Newbury, the doctor's father, he was flipping through the pages when a piece of paper fell out. It looked old and was tattered round the edges carefully he unfolded and then read the contents of the letter. He felt like the one he was intruding but he kept reading. It was a note to he doctor from his father. He was apologising for an accident that happened in has lab when the doctor was a toddler. He blamed himself for turning his back to answer the phone and he never noticed that his son had toddled through the open door and knocked over a test tube of solution that the Professor had been working on. At the time, he did not know that his son had drunk some of the liquid. It was when he started puberty that they realised something was wrong. The Professor had tried to reverse the effects but to no avail. It was too much for him and he took his own life. Graham had wandered round the study looking for more information about the doctor's problems. He opened the drawers of the big desk that sat in one of corners there was not much on the desk just a scribble pad, a pen and pencil. There was no photo is anywhere, there was not much pictures on the wall neither. Overall, the place looked rather bare. He opened the bottom drawer and pulled out a battered diary. He opened it up, looking roughly at the scribbles but there was nothing of interest. That was until he came to the middle of it, there was a photo of a baby wrapped in a white blanket the baby had almost transparent skin. You could see the tiny blue veins on the baby's face. There was a small ginger curl sticking out from under the blanket. There was a letter beside the photo. He unfolded it and read the letter. It was from a woman who was writing to thank him for sorting the DNA results. Her husband had not accepted the child was his and she did not want anyone to find out about them, not yet she had enclosed the photo of their son. They would work something out. The marriage had been over but they were still living together, but that is all. There were no sexual feelings. They had had problems ever since the death of their first child Carla. Life had been stressful, but they tried to patch things up. Nevertheless,things would never have been the same again. They decided that since they had another baby they would stay together for the sake of the baby and the business. Things had been fine. There had been a glimmer of hope and it looked like things were going to sort themselves out. However, there was a huge row and that is when the woman turned to the doctor. He knew that if all the information he had he would be able to cash infrom whoever the husband was.

Luck would have it he had found out that the family were the Costello family that had a string of coffee shops. He plotted his next move very carefully. He watched them found out where they went, whom there friends were and when he had enough information he thought about how he would get a message to Mr Costello about his wife and the DNA results. He heard that they were heading out of town to attend a funeral of a friend. How easy was this he thought? He would follow them slip a note to Mr Costello asking him to meet up as he had some information that he would be interested in concerning the DNA results concerning his son.

He asked a waiter to slip the note to Mr Costello when he was alone. The waiter did. He then asked another waiter to give a parcel to Mr Costello when he was alone. Inside the package was a note asking him to give his wife the sleeping tablets that he had put into the parcel, as she would stop him from coming to the meeting place.

He had asked him to meet him up at the lake a few miles from the hotel, which they were staying at; he wanted them to meet at six whilst it was still dark so no one would see them. He was going to knock out Mr Costello and put them into his jeep then takes them to his father's cottage. He did not need to worry about his father using it as he was out of the country. He knew that his father would be away for the next six months away for six months. Graham went to the lake about five he wanted to make sure that there was no one there and that Mr Costello came alone. He parked his jeep at the far end of the car park, so that he could see if anyone else came in., he waited. About five to six he spotted headlights light up the dark sky. He shifted uneasy in the seat it was all about to happen and he hopped that his plans were foolproof. His car turned into the car park and parked and the middle, the driver then turned the lights off. Graham waited a few minutes then he picked up a bottle that he had hid in his glove box. He soaked the contents of the bottle onto some cotton wool. He disconnected the interior light so that when he opened the door there was no light to give his hiding place away. He slowly opened the door, slid out of the jeep, and crept towards the waiting car. From a distance, he could see that it was Mr Costello and when he got closer, he saw his wife slumped in the passenger seat. Mr Costello was trying to straighten her up. The journey here must have a bumpy ride and she had slipped down. Whilst he was attending to her Graham opened the back driver door. Mr Costello startled as Graham jumped into the car. Graham pulled Mr Costello back into the driver seat and covered his mouth and nose with the soaked cotton wool. Mr Costello struggled and Graham had to try very hard to keep him in the car, twice he managed to open the door, and once he managed to drop the cotton wool. Eventually he managed to detain Mr Costello, after a few moments his body stopped struggling, and he slouched over the steering wheel. Graham ran back to get the jeep, and pulled it along side the Costello's car. He managed to get Mrs Costello into the jeep quite easily but he struggled with the weight of Mr Costello. He saw the dawn breaking and he knew that he needed to hurry. With one final attempt, he eventually got Mr Costello into the back of the jeep. He got into their car and started it up he reversed it and then he drove it towards the lake. He waited until it was close to the water then he jumped clear. He rolled clear of the car and he heard the splash as the car ploughed into the lake. As he walked back towards the jeep he kept looking over his shoulder, as if to check that the car was in fact sinking and not going to is half submerged. He jumped in to the jeep and watched the last few bubbles break the waters surface. He started the jeep, left the car park, and headed to his fathers cottage.

When he reached the cottage, Mrs Costello was starting to come out of her sleep as the effects of the sleeping tablets started to wear off. He scouted the area first before he drove up the front of the cottage. He opened the door to the cottage and made sure that it was empty. He returned to the jeep, carried Mrs Costello into the cottage, and went into one of the bedrooms where he laid her down on the bed. He got a pair of handcuffs {he managed to acquire them when a police cadet left them lying around at the labs} he cuffed her to the bed then he tied her ankles with a piece of cloth he got from the kitchen. He went back to the jeep to get Mr Costello. He opened the back door and pulled the blanket of him. He knew right away that something was wrong. Mr Costello was a grey colour his lips were blue and he was foaming from his mouth. Graham checked for a pulse. He could feel the colour draining from his own face, as he could not find any. He looked at his eyes they were glazed and lifeless. Graham was physically sick. He started to panic. What he was going to do with the body He run his hands through his hair as he paced up and down. He covered the body up and went back into the cottage. He had to get rid of the body. However, he had to make sure that no one was going to find it. He thought for a few moments. He went to a small room behind the kitchen. Here was where his father had kept his fishing, guns, and maps of the area. He rummaged around until he found the one he was looking for. This map covered an area about twenty miles from here. He did not want to dump the body close to the cottage. He studied the map and plotted out where he could get rid of the body so that no one would find the body. He went to the kitchen put the kettle on, checked that Mrs Costello was still alive; he did not want another body on his hands.

Chapter 31

Andrea had woken to find that her hands and feet tied the bedpostsshe struggled but the cloth tied round her ankles was quite tight and she could not free herself. The cuffs tightened when she tugged her hands to free them. She called out for help but no one came. Andrea looked around the small room she was alone where was Julian her husband. She called out for him but there was no reply. Where was he? She tried to remember where she had been but her head felt like if was full of cotton wool. She was thirsty as well she shouted for help but there was still no reply. She waited for a few minutes more them she shouted a lot louder. She heard someone moving about. She wondered if they were going to kill her. Where was Julian was this his idea of a joke, because right now she did not find it funny. The door opened and a stranger stood in the doorway. He was tall and had to bow his head to get through the door. He never spoke. He just walked over to the bed. Unlocked one side of the cuffs and handed her a glass of water. She was unsure about drinking it, as she did not know if it was just water or if there was something in it.

"Where is my husband? I would like to see him please" she asked the man.

He looked at her and said, "Drink this".

"What is it?" she asked.

"It's only water" he replied.

She took the glass and lifted it to her lips she sniffed the contents

"Its only water" he growled.

She slowly sipped the water. There was a funny taste but she was not sure if it was the water or the taste was in her mouth. However, she was thirsty and decided that her thirst needed quenched. The man left and she soon fell asleep.

Chapter 32

Graham drove to the most secluded spot he could find on the map. It was about fifteen miles from the cottage.He was sure that no one would find the body. He hoped that no one would ever find the body.He covered it up with some branches and leaves then he headed back to the cottage. He stopped at a chip shop on the way back. He bought some fish and chips. He drove up the small drive to the cottage and his lights lit up the side of the cottage. They were the only light for miles around. He entered the cottage and drew the curtains in all of the rooms before he switched on the lights. He took one of the fish and chips to the bedroom for Mrs Costello. He knocked on the door. When he heard nothing he opened the door, he started to panic the last thing he wanted was another body. Even worse would be if she managed to escapeHe switched on the light and was relieved to see that she was still there and even more relieved to hear her speak. He went over to her, took one side of the cuffs of, and handed her the fish and chips. She did not realised how hungry she was until she started to eat. He left the room, went into the kitchen, and put the kettle on. He sat at the small table and rubbed his face with his hands.

"How could things go so wrong? Christ everything in my life is so complicated". He mumbled to himself.

He had to get things sorted but he did not know what to do. If he let Mrs Costello go, she would go to the police and then they would be looking for him then the police would charge him with kidnap and murder. He him could flee the country but he was sure that some one would derive a conclusion and then there would be a hunt on for him. Frustration grew deep within him and he could feel it rising from the pit of his stomach. He went into the drawer under the draining board and got the key to the cupboard in the small room where his father kept his hunting and fishing equipment. He opened the cupboard and pulled out a shotgun he picked up a box that contained some cartridges and went back into the kitchen. He went to the cupboard under the sink and pulled out an old shoebox. He took it over to the table and laid it beside the shotgun. He made himself a strong black coffee and sat down at the table. He stared at the gun lying there. He tried to suppress the frustration that he felt. He tried to slow his breathing down. God knows how many times he had counted to ten. He tried to clear his mind. Slowly he closed his eyes and tried to reach the place in his mind where he was calm and happy he nearly got there when he was disturbed by a high-pitched scream. For a moment he was confused what was that noise and where was it coming from. He looked around and it slowly all came back to him. He picked up the shotgun and headed in the directions of the screams.

Andrea had woken to find a rat or a mouse crawling over her she did not know which it was she had only seen the tail and felt it as it ran over her bare legs. She screamed at the top of her lungs. She felt sick and she had broken out in a sweat. How she hated them those vermin. She would not allow any of her children have any pets that lived in a cage and had any resemblance to mice or rats. She froze as the door burst open and the stranger stood in the doorway with a gun under his arm. She thought that this was it. He was going to shoot her. The stranger just stood there and stared at her for a moment. There was no movement; the two of them stared at each other. Just like two baddies would stare at each other waiting, on the other making a move, before there was a shooting and one or both of them would be killed. Only difference was that Andrea did not have a gun. The stranger was not going to say anything so Andrea said in a rather shaky voice, "there was a rat or a mouse here beside me I felt it, crawling over my legs. I am sorry but I have a phobia with them"

He moved over to where she lay on the bed he looked up and down. He even looked under the bed but there was nothing there.

"You must have scared it away with that wailing like a banshee. Because I can not see anything, there is nothing there now". He spoke with gruffness in his voice.

She needed a drink and asked if he could get her something. She talked to him but her eyes never left the gun that he had draped over his arm. He glares back at her for a moment then backed out of the room.

When she was, alone she let out a huge sigh of relief, but wonders if she would be luck the next time she saw the gun. She prayed that it was something that she never saw again. She just got herself calmed down when the door burst open and Graham in carrying a mug with something hot in it she watched him walk towards her with steam rising out of the top of the mug. It looked very inviting to her she could not remember the last time she had had a hot drink. Graham placed the mug on the bedside table and un-cuffed one of her hands so that she could drink her tea.

Graham sat at the kitchen table and tried to figure out his next move. There was certainly going to be no money.Andrea already knew about the DNA tests. However, would she know about the doctor's accident in the lab when he was a toddler? Bet she did not, it is not something that you would tell people "oh and by the way I'm a freak"

He decided that he was going to look at her boy and the doctor more closely. Perhaps there is money here after all. He smiled to himself. He went back to the bedroom, took the mug away, and put the cuffs back on Andrea's wrists. He left the room and went further down the hall to another bedroom and soon he fell asleep dreaming of a suitcase full of money.

Chapter 33

It had been two days since the discovery body of Julian Costello on a remote hillside by an unfortunate farmer, who was out looking over his flock of sheep. The detective could remember taking the phone call from the farmer. He was in a state of shock as he tried to relate the findings of a body on his land. He said that he had been out checking his flock when he stumbled across the body after he thought the smell coming from a small ditch was one of his missing sheep that had died. He looked down into the ditch expecting to see the remains of a sheep, but unfortunately, he got the shock of his life to see the rotten remains of a body. He had returned down the hillside to his farm where he phoned the police. The police promptly arrived and cordoned of the area. Men in white suits came and set up a tent around where the body lay. There was a swarm of police in the area. The farmer had questioned be the detective for three hours. However, he could throw no light on how long the body had lain there. He had only put his sheep out on the hillside two days ago but they had not gone that far up until today. He told the detective that the person who left the body would either have had to have help or the use of an off road vehicle like a quad or something similar. The detective took notes. Then he left the farmer and headed up the hillside to where the forensics was. He listened to the forensics one of them had said that he thought the body was that of Julian Costello he recognised the body even though it was quite decomposed. He spoke to the top man in forensics to see if he had anything, he could tell him. "Off the record" he said, "one of the boys had found tyre tracks. That had come over the hill from the other side and that they had deeper tracks coming up the hill than it left when it went down. A person has been down to check the tread on the farmer vehicles, and asks if there was any one other than himself used the hill. We also have some footprints left by someone's shoes, but we are not holding our breath on that one, we think that they will belong to the body".

"What do you mean belong to the body? How do you come to that conclusion"?

The forensic person gave him a look that told him that he had just asked the dumbest question of the year. However, the detective just stared at him waiting for his explanation.

The forensic cleared his throat then answered

"Well if you look at the feet of the body you will see that there are no shoes on his feet, and"

He spread the palms of his hands upwards and moved them outwards

"As you can see there are no shoes in the area. Now if the person that did this did not want to leave any evidence he would have used the dead person's shoes so that there was none of his footprints. Or any other evidence left at the scene"

He stared back at the detective, who asked,

"So we have a clever guy," he said.

"Yet to meet someone who is cleverer than forensics. Nowadays all we need is a strand of hair or a drop of sweat, blood or saliva. Could even get results from particles of fabric we will get the man, may take time but we will get him" Replied the forensic.

The detective hung about, scrounging cups of coffee. From anyone who he saw drinking. He sat in one of the vans watching the police and the forensics going about their business. He watched for the young copper coming up from the farm. He wanted to know if the farmer had told him anything different from what he had told him. He was watching the white suited men coming and going from the tent that they had erected and thought that they had a gruesome job they had to do. He himself had found some horrific sights but in this part of the country, they were very rare. The worst thing that he had to deal with was a body that was trapped inside a warehouse when had gone on fire. There was a body found inside the burnt out building. Forensics took about a week to identify the remains of the body and it turned out to be a young homeless lad. Whom we believed had fallen asleep then had been over come by the smoke. No one ever came forward to identify or claim the body. Therefore, the people of the village had put a collection round to give the lad a decent burial. His grave is in the local graveyard and some one puts flowers and keeps the plot nice. That thought to himself how kind hearted the people in this area was. But he looked over to the tent where the forensics were doing there job and trying to piece together enough information on who did this to Julian Costello and his family, who were the most respected people that he knew of in the district. A shiver ran the full length of his spine when he had an image of the body lying in the ditch. He thought to himself who on this earth could do something so terrible to a person like Julian. He did not know the Costello's personally but through his line of work had heard so much about them.

There was a loud knock on the door to his office. He jumped almost knocking a cup of coffee all over his desk.

"Come in" he growled.

The door opened and Patrick, the head of the forensics burst through the door.

"I have got the reports from the Costello case. The boys have worked solid since the body was identified" Said Patrick.

He tossed a brown folder on to the detective's desk. The detective looked up at Patrick as he reached over to pull the folder towards him. He opened it and started to read the forensics findings.

Chapter 34

James had left the girls at the kitchen table and headed to his room. He opened his bedroom door and hesitated. He was bored. He had been cooped up in the house for what seemed like an eternity, even though it had been only been four days. Then that was an eternity to an outdoor lad like James. He closed the door and headed along the corridor, to a door that was opposite his parent's bedroom. He stood between them. He was going to head up the stairs to the attic but he now wanted to go into their bedroom. He opened the door very slowly; it was as if he was afraid of what he might find behind the door, his mind started to work overtime. What if his mum was in there lying dead. Perhaps the person that killed their father might have put her body in there. She might be laying on the bed her body rotten with her flesh crawling with maggots. Her long black hair matted with her blood. He stood at the door unsure of whether to enter the bedroom or shut the door and wait to see if anyone else would be brave enough to go into his parent's bedroom. He thought for a moment, if there were a dead body in there surly, there would be a smell. He closed his eyes and opened the door a bit further he took a small sniff. However, he could not smell anything. He did not know what a dead body should smell like but he assumed that that it would be a terrible smell, worse than his old trainers did. There was no terrible smell just the smell of his mums perfume and a hint of his father's aftershave. He decided that it was safe to go in, as there were no bad smells only good ones. He slowly opened one eye and squinted round the room when he was sure that it was all clear he opened the other. Everything was tidy and there was certainly no body here. He walked over to the dressing table. A photo of them all that had been taken last year when they went on holiday he remembered the man approaching them as the wandered round a street market. He asked if they wanted there photograph taken to remind them of their holiday. His father objected saying that they did not need a photo to remember them of there holiday, he would only need to look at his bank statement. He remembers his mum digging their father in the ribs and saying,

"Don't be an old grump; it would be nice of them to have a photo of them all together. Smiling" she added.

The photographer arranged them.

"Say cheese"

He wondered why you had to say cheese. It had nothing to do with photography. He looked at the photo. His mum looked so relaxed her hair was immaculate. She always looked like a film star. He thought that she would look good in a movie. He could imagine her playing the part in a romantic film crying as her lover had gone to fight for his country. Leaving her alone, waiting on him. Not knowing wither he would be killed in action. Waiting on his return. Marrying her and living happily after. He looked at his father he looked tired and grumpy he was always grumpy. He wondered how his mum put up with him. He was always shouting and it seemed to be at him more than Jack, or the twins. As he looked at the smiling faces of the twins and Jack he saw for the first time how different he was. They had dark hair and their eyes were greenish brown colour. Their skin had a colouring to it not like his. He had the whitest skin he had ever seen. He knew before that he was a bit different from the rest of the family. However, today was the first he realised just how different he was. He stared at the photo for a few moments he could his eyes start to burn. He put the photo back where he got it and left the room. He crossed the corridor opened the door to the attic and climbed the stairs. He had not been up here by himself and at first; it was as scary as walking into his parent's bedroom. He stood at the top of the stairs and looked around. There were old prams; he could remember the twins getting pushed around in them when they were babies there was boxes of old clothes. He could see old toys that he had played with. He walked into the middle of the room. It was very dusty. He pulled a cover of off a rocking horse that had been in his room until a few years ago. He watched the dust particles dance in the sunlight that shone through the small skylight on the roof. He walked over to a large desk that was on the furthest away wall. He pulled the chair out and sat in front of the large desk. He felt like a lawyer or a boss of a large company making very important decisions. He soon forgot about the photo. How different he was from the rest of the family. He played around with the bits of paper and things that were on the desk. He opened up the roll top compartment and opened one of the drawers. Inside there was bits of paper he opened some of them up and read them some were receipts from the coffee shops they were very old he read the date. He was amazed to find out that the bit of paper he held in his hands was older than him. He carefully folded it and put it back in the drawer. As he played, he opened drawers. Unfolded, read. Then he refolded the bits of paper… He tried to open one of the drawers. This drawer, unlike the rest of drawers it was locked. At first, he did not bother about it. He went on reading the things that were lying around. He was about to leave the desk when he decided that he was a secret agent and the documents that he needed were in the locked drawer. He crept back to the door and checked that the coast was clear. He went back to the desk and tried to open the locked drawer. He looked around the desk to see where the key that open the drawer could be. He kept checking over his shoulder just as the secret agents did in the films he watched on the telly. The thought he heard a noise so just like the secret agents on the television he hid behind a stack of boxes and waited to see if anyone came up the stairs. He tried to remember if he had closed the door. If he had not then if anyone came, upstairs then he or she would see the door was open and they might come up to see what was going on. He crept towards the top of the stairs in the attic and looked down. He sighed as he realised that he had in fact closed the door behind him. If he wanted to be a super secret agent then he would have to make sure that he covered his tracks. He walked back over to the desk and tried to open the locked drawer again. He was finding it very hard to open. He looked around and found a screwdriver. He prised open the drawer without doing to much damage. He looked inside the drawer and was disappointed to find that the contents were pieces of paper. The was going to shut the drawer but then decided that if the drawer was the only one to be locked and the others were open, then perhaps there might be something interesting in there after all. He picked up all the pieces of paper and placed them on the desk. He unfolded the first one it was just more receipts from the shop. He rummaged through some more but there was nothing interesting they were old receipts. At the bottom of the pile, he came across a bit of paper that looked different from the rest. This piece in quarters, not like the others they in half. He unfolded and read the top line Dearest Andrea. That was his mums name the frowned. Who would write a letter to his mum?

Then he smiled as he thought it must have been his dad. It might be a love letter from when they first met. He read a few more lines, he felt as if he was snooping, but curiosity got the better of him and he read more. At first, it was just a lot of how he was missing her and he hoped that he could still see her. James was thinking that perhaps they had split up and this was he asking her to come back. He paused for a moment. He looked more closely at the writing. This was not his dads. The writing on the letter was small and tidy, and clearly written. His dad's writing was scribbles and always looked like it was written quicklyCuriosity got the better of him and he sat down on the chair beside the desk and read the whole letter when he had finished he wished that he had not. It seemed too been have written from someone that his mother had been seeing behind his dad's back. In addition, as there was no date on the letter he had no idea how long ago it had happened. Nor did he know if his mum was still seeing this person. He looked at the remainder of bits of paper and decided that it would be best to put them back in the drawer and leave the attic. Perhaps he would forget the things that he had just read, more likely they would eat away at him.

Chapter 35

James headed back down the stairs to the kitchen. It seemed very quiet, which was not normal, usually when the twins were at home; there was always a noise somewhere in the house. As he went into the kitchen, he heard voices coming from the front room. He heard someone's voice but could not make out what he was saying. Then he heard Mary speaking. He was going to listen at the door but remembered the letter and changed his mind. He went trough the kitchen to a cupboard in a clock room at the back door. He opened the door and took out the doctors fishing gear. He went outside to his little shed in the corner of the garden. This was his shed and he sometimes came here to escape from the house when it got to noisy. He unlocked the door and went inside. He had made it quite comfortable. There was an easy chair and a small table. He had collected quite a few tools and other bits and bobs. He kept his fishing gear here and he had assortments of rods, hooks, flies, reels. Nearly everything you could think of, he had in his shed. He closed the door and laid the doctors gear on the table.

He reached under the table and pulled out a bright red plastic box. He opened it, pulled out a load of cloths, started to dismantle the doctor's fishing rod, and started to clean it. He kept thinking about the letter that he had read. He wondered how long his mother had kept the letter. He also wondered why. He wondered what the person would be like. He thought if his mum had stopped seeing this person and started to see his father then he must have been bad. He started to think about the way his father had been with him. For as long as he could remember his father had been different towards him. He would not take him out as much as he had taken Jack out; they had gone to watch movies, football games he even took Jack fishing. Jack seemed to get all his fathers attention. He had grown up with it and had accepted it. Now it seemed to keep coming to his mind more often. He looked out of the small window and wished that his mum were here. He prayed for her safety. He felt so alone here without her. He could feel his eyes sting as the tears filled his eyes. He sniffed and used his sleeve to wipe away the tears. He gave a crooked smile as he looked at the tear stained marks on his sleeve as he heard his mum tut and say

"That's not what sleeves are for now is it"

He looked over his shoulder hoping to see her smiling at the door. He was disappointed to see that there was no one in the shed but himself. He sniffed and returned to the cleaning of the doctors fishing gear. Perhaps if the weather was good at the weekend they could put the new boat in the water and take it for a test run. Mary could pack a picnic and they all could have a day out. There would be some of the men at the harbour would take the boat out and show him how to sail it. That is if the doctor did not know how to sail her. He had made up his mind that the boat was a she. In addition, he would think of a good name to call her. He spent quite a lot of time on the fishing gear and when he had finished he tidied away all the things he had been using and then stored the Doctors rods beside his own. He locked the shed and headed back to the house. Doctor Newbury was sitting at the table with the detective when he walked in. Both stopped talking when he opened the door he looked at the doctor who gave him a faint smile and said

"Mary is in the front room with the twins their having a small snack at the moment. Jack is out at Beth's house and when he phones, we will all go out for tea, the treats on me. I need to talk with the detective but I will join you when we are finished. Okay".

James nodded at the doctor then he looked at the detective and asked,

"Have you found my mum yet"?

The detective saw the hurt in the boy's eyes and he felt his pain he could not answer him so he lowered his head and shook his head. The doctor noticed the detective is unease and quickly replied,

"They are working on it as best as they can at the moment".

James never took his eyes of the detective, which made him more uncomfortable, and said,

"She could be laying dead somewhere or injured needing help and you're sitting here drinking afternoon tea with the doctor why aren't you looking for her".

The tears had sprung to his eyes again but this time he could not stop them.

He turned and ran towards the door as the detective stood up and said

"Son are doing all we can"

Whether James heard him, he will never know as James never stopped or looked back. The doctor asked the detective to sit down and continue with their discussion. He would go and see to James when they had finished their discussion.

The detective had come to ask the doctor more about the death or rather murder of Julian Costello. The forensics had found traces of chloroform in some of the blood and tissue is that they had taken from Julian's body. It also appears that Julian had had an allergic reaction to the chloroform and that is what caused his death. When the doctor heard the detective say what had caused the death of Julian he shifted uneasy in his seat he stared at the table as he recalled the time that he had preformed the ligament operation on Julian. Julian had just been anesthetised him when the machines monitoring his vital signs started to bleep. He had to act fast so that Julian did not die on the operating table. He had used chloroform before with no adverse reaction but this time he had taken an allergic reaction to the drug. They managed to revive him and he had been under observation for twenty-four hours with no lasting damage. The detective tapped his shoulder and jolted him back to the presence.

"We would like to see Mr Costello's medical records please. I will send one of the lads round to the clinic and he could pick them up" the detective said or rather ordered.

"Yes that won't be a problem. His notes will be available for you. It is on his records when I did the operation on his knee he had taken a reaction to the chloroform we had used. When I think about it him"

The doctor stopped talking as he realised that what he was about to say could get him into a whole lot of trouble. The doctor pushed back his chair and went to the hall to use the phone. When he came back into the kitchen the detective was in the middle of making him another cup of coffee.

He said "he what"

"Pardon" the doctor asked.

Just before you got up to use the phone, you said, "When I think about it him. You didn't finish so I'm asking you again he what"

The doctor looked at the detective and shifted guiltily from one foot to the other, just like a pupil that had being naughty in the class.

Realising that he was feeling that way he coughed and then replied

"I was about to say that he must have been to a dentist and they would have used chloroform. However, he never said anything about having problems there. And we never had any one else having problems."

He waited to see if the detective had any thing to say but he just pulled himself up from the table and headed for the door. He turned and asked,

"Will Mr Costello's notes be waiting for me?"

"\yes I've told them to have them ready for you ton pick up today. But you will have to sign the book to say that you have taken them from the clinic."

The two walked to the front door in silence the doctor a few paces behind the detective, his forehead wrinkled and a rather worried look in his eyes. When they reached the front door the detective turned to the doctor and said a bit sarcastically

"Enjoy your tea".

However, the doctor just nodded and opened the door to let the detective out of the house. He stood long after the detective had gone staring out into no-where. The loud shrill from the telephone jolted his back to the hall. He turned and headed towards the phone. He picked it up. It was Jack needing picked up from Beth's house in about an hour. The doctor said that they would all head out for something to eat when he came to pick him up. Jack agreed and asked if he could bring Beth. Then when they had eaten, hecould take her home later on. The doctor agreed and he knew by the tone in his voice that he was a good deal happier than when he had left him earlier. They chatted for a few minutes and then they said their good-bys. He hung the phone up and went to tell Mary and the twins that they were leaving in about forty minutes to pick up Jack and Beth then go and get something to eat. The girls squealed with excitement whether it was they were going out to eat or that they were picking up Beth. He knew that they looked up to Beth and it had been a while since they had seen her. They left the room chatting excitably about what they were going to wear. He told Mary why the detective had been round. She looked interested but deep down he knew that the medical terms that he used had gone right over her head. He said that James had come in and was upset and that he was going to see him and make sure that he was okay. He left the room and headed up the stairs taking two at a time. He was quite surprised that he was not out of breath when he reached the top landing. He knocked on James's bedroom door and waited for an answer. There was an uneasy silence he opened the door slowly. He was a bit concerned that James had not answered. The lad had been upset when he came in; perhaps he should have gone to make sure that he was all right sooner. The room was in darkness. The curtains in the room were drawn. There was an eerie silence. The only noise that he could here was the ticking of James's alarm clock. "James, James is you there" he asked concern growing.

He fumbled at the wall to try to find the light switch. It clicked throwing the room into brightness he had to blink a few times. He scanned the room. The bed was unmade and James's clothes thrown across the room but there was no sigh of James. He was relieved, though it was only temporarily. He had to find James he hoped that the lad had not done anything silly. He flicked out the light and closed the door. He went down the hall to the door that led into Andrea and Julian's bedroom. He paused at the door before knocking and calling out for James. When there was no reply, he opened the door and popped his head round the door to see if he was in here. The room was one that would not have looked out of place in a house and home magazine he looked around there was no sighing of James. He went in and closed the door behind him. He could smell Andrea; her perfume was as strong as if she was right behind him. Sub consciously he looked over his shoulder. He walked over to her dressing table. He picked up her hairbrush. He pulled some of Andrea's strands of hair, which the hairbrush had entwined in its bristles. He rolled them between his fingers. He looked up and saw a photo of her and the kids. She looked so happy and relaxed. The photo looked like it had been taken in the summer, the sky was bright and cloudless it looked like it was the festival of the sea day there was stalls behind them and he could see the sea queen sitting on her throne with the king and all her page boys standing at her side. He smiled. He remembered the year when James played the sea king He had been so excited he had been rehearsing for weeks. Where he was to go and where he had to stand, he used his sisters to pretend that they were the sea queen and ordered them around until they had got fed up with him and told him that they weren't coming to see him if he didn't stop making them do the silly things he was asking. Dr Newbury remembered standing back from the crowd as the float carrying the sea queen and king made its way from the harbour to the lavishly decorated church hall. He stood at the back of the hall watching them being crowned. He also watched Andrea as she beamed with pride as James was crowned. He could hardly take his eyes of her. She had on a pale pink, almost white, floating summer dress on. The dress showed her tiny waist, as it hugged her, the dress then flared out over her hips and it stopped just below her knee. That showed of her shapely legs.

He loved her whole look and he adored her legs he thought that they were her best feature. Although he thought there was everything about Andrea was her best feature. He put the photo back and wandered over to the beds. They were single and he knew that Andrea had the one nearest the window. She often told him that she looked out at the stars and wondered what he was doing She had said that on a clear night see could see the lights from his house. Every night just before he went to bed, he would flick the lights three times two for a goodnight kiss and one for sweet dreams. He sat down on Andrea's bed and picked up her pillow. He buried his face deep into the pillow and called out her name. He took a deep breath as he felt a lump in his throat he lifted his head up and looked out of the window.

"You could be anywhere, hurt and needing help. God knows you might even be dead lying waiting to be discovered I promised that I would look after you make sure that you were safe. Make sure that on one ever hurt you and now I feel so useless. I do not know where to start looking for you. I pray every minute of the day that you are safe und unhurt. I pray that soon you shall be here where you belong. Back here to the ones that truly loves you".

He closed his eyes and hugged the pillow tightly as if he had Andrea back and never wanted to let her go ever again. He missed the small fluffy feather drift past the window and land on the windowsill.

A sudden bang startled him he dropped the pillow and looked around him. There was nothing or no one around he stood still straining his ears. Waiting to see if there would be anyone appears or thing going to appear. He heard it again this time he realised that it had come from above him.

"The attic "he said out loud "he must be up there in the attic"

He picked up the pillow and put it back on the bed. He left the room and went into the hall. He saw that the door was slightly ajar he went over and opened it. He started to climb the stairs. When he was half way up when he called out to James. "JAMES ARE YOU UP HERE"

He waited but there was no answer .he continued up to the top. At first, he could not see him. Then a movement caught his eye.

"James" he said softly

"James is you alright. I have been looking for you. We are all getting ready to go and get something to eat you ready. James sniffed and then asked

"Why did my father treat me differently from the others did he hate me."

The doctor wanted to take James in his arms and squash the life out of his because he wanted him to know that his father did not hate him. He wanted him to know that his father was proud of him. He wanted to take him to and tell him that everything was going to be all right. However, he could not he promised that he would wait until he was older then he would sit down with Andrea and tell him who his real father was. He could not wait for that day. He wanted Andrea to divorce Julian and come and live with him he would accept the others to unlike Julian.

He would have treated them all the same. He knew that it was up to Andrea but she was unsure. She had long fell out of love with Julian. Her money kept the business going. After Julian had started to gamble and nearly lost everything. She took over the business. It had been difficult and it looked like they were going to loose everything, that was until Doctor Newbury became a silent partner he loaned her the money so that she could keep the business running. And she had done a great job and three years later she had repaid all the money back to the Doctor he still kept a small share hold in the business but never bothered with any of the financial side every year he got a percentage of the profits but that when into an account for James. It was when all the financial breakdown of the business was happening that Andrea told Julian about James. She also told Julian about her affair with the doctor. And she had told Julian that he could walk away from everything but he would never get a penny and the locals would have a field day or they continued to live together and keep the business going and he would get a wage and he would have a car and no-one would ever know. He opted to keep quiet and get a wage. As time went on and the business grew, they both took a wage and got someone in to look after the financial side of the business with Andrea making all the decisions. He looked at the lad sitting on the rocking horse that was far too small for him and said,

"Your father doesn't hate you. Sometimes it is hard for him to show his feelings. He might be different towards you because he does not understand you. Maybe he thinks that because you do not look like him the only way he can deal with it is to treat you different. However, that is not your fault nor is it his he just cannot deal with it. You know. Remember how you felt when you liked the girl that had the leading role in the summer play and you thought that it would be a good thing to get a part just to see her. However, when you saw her you did not know what to say. So you treated her differently"

He looked at James who looked like he was listening. He continued,

"Well that's how you dealt with it and how your father is with you is his way of dealing with you being different. But what I can tell you is that the horse that you're sitting on was made especially for you look"

He pointed to the saddle and showed James the letters J C carver on to the front of it. "And I don't know if you remember but you fell off and banged your head quite badly and he sat with you all night. He held your hand. Remember when you broke your arm. The time that when you fell out of the tree. Your father organised the local football team to come and give you a visit. Do you remember your favourite player came in and signed the cast you had on your arm."

James nodded and he wiped his eyes, looked at the doctor, and asked,

"Is Jack ready. Was that him on the phone?"

"Yes I said that we would pick him and Beth up in about forty five minutes so we better get a move on"

He helped James down from the rocking horse and as they headed for the door, he could not resist ruffling James's hair.

Chapter 36

Mary and the twins were waiting in the front room. The girls were jumping about excitedly, chattering away between themselves. Mary was flicking through a magazine when James and the doctor walked through the door. They all stood up and gathered their coats and bags ready to get loaded up in to the car.

"Mary wills you take the twins in my car and I will take James in Jacks car and we can pick up Jack and Beth and meet you at the town centre and we can decide where we can eat. Tell you what why don't the ladies decide where we eat before we go" said the doctor

The twins and Mary huddled together as they discussed where they were going to eat. James looked at the doctor, was about to say something when he put his arm around James's shoulder, and whispered,

"If you let them decide on where we eat then we can decide on what picture we see. Then we might not end up watching a chick flick. It's tactics".

James thought about what the doctor had just said and when he realised the sneakiest side of it. He smiled and put his hand up for a high five. The doctor obliged and the two of them waited until the women announced that it would be the pizza parlour. The doctor and James looked at each other and smiled and James said to the doctor as they left the room

"It's going to be a good night because I would have picked the pizza parlour. And now we can go and see a film that isn't a"

He pulled a funny face and continued in the worst girl accent possible

"Chick flick"

The doctor laughed as he ushered James out the door. He looked over his shoulder and called

"Come along ladies"

In addition, as the passed, him at the door he bowed. It was like a clip out of a comedy strip. The girls flicked their heads as they passed him and both said,

"Come along Jeeves. Don't keep the ladies waiting it's not proper."

The doctor got the twins into the back of his car and put their belts on put the child locks on and closed the door he opened the front door and waited for Mary who was checking the doors and windows. She eventually hurried towards the car apologising. He waited until she had made herself comfortable and showed her where the lights and gears were then closed the door. He was about to leave to get into Jack's car when he turned back around and knocked on the window. Mary was trying to wind the window down to see what he was wanting. However, it not being her own car was finding it rather difficult. The doctor opened the door smiling to him and said "sorry there electric and the buttons are there."

He pointed to a small switch beside the cigarette lighter on the dashboard. He continued,

"Just take the girls in and ask if you can have a table for six and we will join you as soon as we can".

Mary nodded and looked rather flustered. He put his hand on her shoulder and said, "Calm down. It is only a car. Just like the one, you drive only the make is different. However, every thing is the same, look a steering wheel, in the same place. The pedals all in the same place and in the right order accelerator at the door. The brake is in the middle and the clutch at the far side. You'll be fine just follow me and we'll drive slowly, till you get used to it okay"

Mary laughed and started the car. He doctor closed the door and went over to Jack's car. James was already strapped in and eagerly waiting for the doctor to start the engine. He had only been in the car a few times but the times he had been in it he felt like a superstar. The doctor started the car and eased it slowly out of the drive. Mary followed a short distanced behind. The doctor kept his eye on Mary who was behind him. It was on one of the checks that he noticed the car following them. It was a dark saloon but he could not make out what model. They did see that there were two people in the front. They looked like they were wearing suits. He slowed down to see what they would do. No surprise there he thought to himself they slowed down too. There was a lay-by up a head, he waited until the last minute and indicated and pulled in and hoped that Mary followed him in. She did. He quickly got out of

Jacks car and walked over to Mary who had a puzzled look on her face. He looked along the road and saw the car that had been tailing them parked a short distance away waiting at the side of the road. Mary had managed to open the window and she was about to ask if there was something wrong.He asked her to stay there. He sprinted towards the car that was waiting at the roadside. The occupants of the cargo9t themselves into a fluster as they watched then Doctor running towards their carThey could not drive off as the doctor was running in the middle of the road. In addition, a stream of cars was coming down on the opposite side of the road stopping them from u turning and escaping technically he had them trapped. He approached the dark car, stood in front of it, and shouted

"WHO ARE YOU AND WHY ARE YOU FOLLOWING US. ARE YOU REPORTERS?"

He waited for an answer. The two men in the car looked at each other and he could see that they were discussing something. After a moment or two, the passenger opened the door. The passenger reached inside his coat as got out of the car. For a split second, he thought that perhaps they were the people that had killed Julian and now he was standing between them and the rest of the family. He had been stupid he not only had he put his own life in danger but he had put the rest of the Costello's in danger too. He hoped that there would be too many cars passing, as they would be witnesses if anything happened. Could he make it back to the car and drive off? No that would be stupid if they were armed they would kill him before he reached the car. He stood still as the man started walking towards him, his hand still in the inside of his jacket. The doctor felt the inside of his mouth go dry. He felt his pulse quicken and his breathing got heavy. His insides started to twist. He felt queasy. He thought about shouting to Mary and getting her to drive off but that would leave James stranded. The stranger got closer. He could try to get whatever he had in his pocket. That again was stupid; the other person that was in the car was not going to sit and watched as the Doctor was attacking his accomplice. The traffic had slowed and there was only a few cars passing and the doctor prayed that he would be alive in the morning. The stranger was only a few feet away when he brought his hand out from inside his pocket. He dropped whatever he had in his hand. The doctor saw the opportunity and when the stranger bent down he kicked the stranger he got him square on the head and sent him reeling backwards. The doctor reached down to pick up whatever the stranger had dropped. He looked around but there was not a gun or anything that resembled anything like a gun or a knife. It was just a plastic wallet. He looked at the man rolling about the ground in agony and then at the other man running towards him. He realised at that moment that they were police officers. He put his hands behind his head and waited to see what his fate brought. Whilst the other police officer was coming to the assistance of his colleague, it gave him vital time to think. The two officers were like the key stone cops and Doctor Newbury found it hard to keep from laughing as the two of them tried to get things under control. The one that the doctor had kicked was trying to pick himself up and the other officer who was trying to help kept falling over him. In the end, the doctor went over to where they were; and helped the injured officer to his feet. He checked that there was no serious damage to the officer and then he decided that he would confront them about their hideous skills at undercover work. He picked the driver first.

"Have you ever done any undercover work before because I spotted you the minute you drove out of the parking space you were as obvious as a torch in the dark? In addition, when I stopped you should have drove on not stopped yards from where I pulled in to the lay-by and waited further along the road. Christ I am not a cop and I know that."

He looked straight at them. They were standing staring at the ground. They knew that what he was saying was true they had made a complete shambles or the show so far. "Why are you following us and who gave the orders for you to do it."

The two men looked at each other one frowned and nodded to the other. The driver spoke

"We were asked to keep an eye on the Costello's by the detective. He wants the kids left alone. To make sure that there are no reporters harassing them? He thinks they have a tough enough time."

He lowered his head and mumbled something that the doctor could not make out. "Look up when you speak and stop mumbling. What did you say?" asked the doctor. His patience was running out. The driver spoke again this time he looked right at the doctor and said

"He want's us to keep an eye on you as well."

The driver was obviously unsure how the doctor was going to take the news that he was under surveillance and shifted from one foot to the other.

"Well I am going back to the car and taking the twins and their nanny to the pizza parlour. Dropping them off then I has to pick up Jack and his friend. Then we are all coming back to the parlour to have something to eat. Therefore, if you have to follow me as well as the kids you had better radio in and get assistance. Because we will be heading in different directions shortlynow I'm heading back to my car and heading to the pizza parlour".

With that, he turned around and strode back to the cars. As he passed Mary, he said

"It's okay just a misunderstanding. Let's get some food"

He went to Jack's car started it. Pulled out of the lay-by and headed for town.

They pulled up out side the pizza parlour and they all went in to get a table. The doctor spoke to waiter. Who showed the twins and Mary to a table and then went to the kitchen and returned carrying a plastic carrier bag. He handed it to the doctor. The doctor went to police car, handed the man in the passenger side, and handed the bag to a bewildered looking man and said,

"Keep this on and that lump and it should help the swelling down to a minim. I am of to get Jack you wait here I will manage to keep an eye on the two boys. Wont be long"

He got into Jack's car and drove off down the street. He watched in his rear view mirror but that stayed in the car close to the pizza parlour.

Chapter 37

The seven of them sat at a table at the back of the shop. It was quite quiet. There were a few young couples in but they were at the front of the shop. The incident earlier had made the doctor more aware of who was around. He was thinking what explanation would they give if he asked why he needed observationThere was a few times he let himself become more absorbed in his thoughts. Jack had to give him a nudge to bring him back into the conservation. He excused himself and went to the toilet. Jack gave him a few moments then followed him.

"You seem far away is everything alright? Jack said to the doctor as he exited the toilet. The doctor rubbed his head with his hands and shook his head.

"There was an incident on the way here and it seems that the detective wants you and the kids to have police surveillance. It is for your protection. However, it is for your own safety. Jack looked worried and said, "Are we in danger"

The doctor quickly Said, "No I don't think so if you were I think they would have put you all in a safe house. I think it has more likely been keep the press away and give you some privacy. But I need to let you know."

He paused. After a heavy sigh, he continued, "I am under surveillance. I think that they suspect that I have something to do with the case."

Jack thought for a moment his eyebrows wrinkled deep with concentration. He looked at the doctor and asked; "are you tell the truth."

The doctor looked at Jack and was about to speak when Jack continued in a whisper "I know about you and my mum. However, I also know the situation between my mum and dad. I have known for a while and if you make my mum happy I'm fine with it and I know that my dad had accepted it so I wouldn't think there would be any problems there."

The doctor was a bit surprised that Jack knew about him and his mum. He blushed slightly.

"Jack I would never hurt your mum or dad. I could never kill you dad because I know that, even though they were not in love physically they still cared for each other and if I or anyone killed either of them the would be hurt. So no I promise I have nothing to do with their disappearance nor the murder of your father."

Jack could see the hurt in the doctor's eyes, the pain etched on his face, and he knew that he was telling the truth. He put his hand on the doctor's arm and said,

"I didn't think you had it in you to hurt any of them. Let's get back to the table before they think there's something going on between us."

The doctor laughed at this comment and as Jack led the way back to the table, he could see that he a lot older than his eighteen years. The rest of the group were tucking to a feast of pizza they were all deep in conservation and it looked like they were never missed. They sat down and joined in the feast and the conversation. The evening went quite quick. Jack and the doctor exchanged glances both smiling at each other to let them know that there was still friendship there.

Once the group had finished the feast, they were discussing what they might do next. James was quick to suggest the pictures. He was pleased when everyone agreed. The doctor suggested that since the women had chosen where they ate it was only fair to let the men folk decide on which film they should watch. Everyone except the twins agreed. A protesting Sarah whined, "It'll be that horror movie that has just been released. I heard that it's really gruesome."

She pulled a scary face and everyone laughed.

"Don't worry we wont be watching anything of a horror nature." replied Jack.

The girls gave a sigh off relief.For the next few minutes, there was a lot of chatter about the different movies that were showing. Eventually they had whittled it down to two.Which was what the boys wanted to see? On the other hand, a romantic one, which was what girls wanted to see. They decided that they would drive to the cinema and see if what would happen. The doctor went to pay the bill and the women all trouped of to the toilet. Jack and James finished their drinks then followed the doctor.

"Why?" James piped up.

"Why is it that when one female needs the toilet that all the other females in the group have to go at the same time?"

The doctor and Jack both laughed at the same time.

"The greatest minds in the world have tried and failed to answer that very question you have asked. It remains on of the great mysteries of the world. And the person who can solve it will be up there with the greatest of men forever more." replied the doctor.

"But they seem to spend ages in there. What do they do? I think anyone who spends that amount of time in a toilet needs help." James said pulling a face of disgust.

Jack agreed with him. The three of them waited patiently on the girls returning form the toilet. They had begun to think that perhaps they had been stuck. James asked the doctor if he would go and check they were all right.

He replied, "Perhaps I might"

He started to move when the four females emerged from the toilet giggling. Jack held the door opened and let everyone out. They all jumped into the cars and headed to the cinema. The doctor let Jack drive his car and he let James sit in the front. He sat behind Jack from here he could see the rear view mirror. He kept checking what cars were following them. The only one was that of the keystone cops. This did not bring peace of mind.

They stood in front of the information boards in the foyer of the cinema looking at what films were showing. They still could not decide on one film. In the end, the girls opted to see the romantic movie and the boys opted to see the action movie. They were waiting to pay when Jack pulled James to one side and asked him

"Would you be upset if I went to see the romantic movie with Beth? We are going to make a go of it. I'll make it up to you promise?"

James looked at his brother as if he had lost all his marbles then said, "Glad I don't have a girlfriend. It must be embarrassing having to sit and watch soppy movies with a girl crying and all that. You can sit with her I do not mind. But I'm going to think on how you can make it up to me" he joked with Jack.

"I know what I'll do just you wait here and keep your eyes shut. Promise me." Jack said.

He took off before James could say anything. James closed his eyes and waited. He waited for what seemed an eternity. James was starting to thinking he been left to standing there when as the others went to watch the film. When he heard, Jack shouts

"HOPE YOU ARE KEEPING THOSE EYES CLOSED."

James squeezed his eyes tighter. He could hear Jack panting at his side and the rustling of paper.

"Wait a moment. Not ready yet." panted jack.

James could not wait to open his eyes. He wondered what Jack had for him. Perhaps it was the biggest tub of popcorn the cinema had. However, that would be a shame because he did not have room in his stomach to eat it after all that pizza. After a few moments Jack gave him the order him to "open them now."

James opened them and blinked a few times. At first, he could not see what Jack had brought him.

He could not even see Jack. He started to think that it was a sick joke his brother had played on him. He stared at the ground. He could feel the tears prick his eyes. He looked up to see if he could see the rest of the group when Jack jumped from behind large cardboard cut out of the hero in the film they were about to see.

"Look what I got you I know how much you idolise this chap so I spoke to that chap over there" he pointed to a man dressed in a uniform.

Who saw them and waved.

"And he said that as this was the last showing of the film I could have this" Jack beamed pointing to the cardboard cut out.

James could only stare at the large cut out. Never could he imagine getting anything like this. He was already thinking about where in his bedroom it should take pride of place.

" the man's going to look after it till the movies over then we will load it in to one of the cars and then you can take it home" Jack said the smile still ear to ear.

Jack had made James's night. He had him a life size figure of his hero. Ever since James saw Conrad Ledgers in an action film two years ago fighting the baddies. Swimming in shark infested waters. Hanging dangerously to the side of a speeding train. The best bit was when Conrad had to ride a motor bike off a mountain. James thought that Conrad was going to die.

However, he managed to land in the sea and survived. He will remember the end of that film forever. The whole cinema cheered and James's cheers were the loudest. Now this was going to be the best he was going to see the latest movie starring his hero Conrad then later he was going to have the world's best actor in his bedroom. How could anyone be scared at night when the he had Conrad Ledger was protecting them. James thought he was the luckiest boy in the world. His brother had done well.

No, he thought again he had done excellent.

The film that the women were watching had finished first and they were waiting on the action film finishing. Jack and Beth had gone to find the man who was looking after Conrad for them. The twins helped position Conrad so that he looked like he was greeting James as he emerged from the darkness on the room. Emma started to swoon over him. Which amused Mary and Beth? Once every one was in place, they waited patiently on the film finishing. James and the doctor emerged from the darkness to see Conrad and the rest of the group waiting. Jack was standing at the side of the cut out and did his best to mimic Conrad voice. Although it wasn't very good but a few of the other film goers laughed and James felt like royalty as people looked, some with jealousy others with amusement. The doctor suggested that they all headed back to the Costello's so that they could get every one including Conrad home without being crushed. James wanted to be in the same car as Conrad. When they put Conrad in the doctor's car James quickly jumped in. Jack laughed as James ordered one of the twins to sit in the front. He commented to the doctor "he must be in love. He never lets a chance to sit in the front pass him by"

Both men laughed at the joke and waited until everyone had found a seat.

"You lead and I'll follow. However, remember that you have more horsepower than I do. Oh and do not worry if a third car joins our party. Laurel and Hardy have a job to do" he nodded towards the car parked close.

"No problem" replied Jack see you at the house.

All three cars left the car park and headed towards the Costello's home.

Chapter 32

James raced up the stair with Conrad and there were a few bangs before all went quiet. "I take it that Mr Ledger had his place in James's room," Mary announced as she came into the room carrying a tray with glasses of warm milk and cookies.

"Do you mind if I take Beth home first. I can get mine when I return," asked Jack.

"No that's will not a problem. It was nice to see you again Beth. We have had a lovely evening. Girls Beth is going home come and say good-by."

Mary hugged Beth. Then left the room and shouted for James to come and say good-by to Beth. James appeared at the door and ran into Beth's arms he gave her the biggest hug he had and whispered,

"Glad your back. I've missed you."

She squeezed him and whispered back

"Glad to be back I've missed you more."

She released her grip on him and ruffled his hair.

"Look after Conrad. I'll pop round soon promise"

She took his hand and they walked towards the front door. Jack was already in the car waiting. Beth hugged James again and said good-bye to everyone. Jumped into the car and as they drove away the doctor shouted,

"Drive carefully."

James watched and wave until the taillights had vanished.

The doctor was in the kitchen talking to Mary

"I need to check James's leg. It should almost be healed I was amazed at the way he heals."

Mary asked if he wanted to check it tonight.

"Yes if James doesn't mind," answered the doctor.

"Don't think he will mind. I think he is desperate for a bath. He asked if he could have one earlier."

The doctor said to Mary "go and run him a bath and we can check the wound. I think a bath will not hurt him"

Mary disappeared and the doctor went to get James from the front room. He opened the door and found him chatting with the twins.

"James got another surprise for you"

James turned round and had a puzzled look on his face.

The twins looked even more puzzled.

"It's okay. I just wondered if I could have a look at your leg and perhaps if it looks good you and have a bath"

The doctor said quickly as it looked like the puzzled looks were about to turn to worried looks.

"Can we see your leg?" Sarah asked.

"I thought that you didn't like horror things "laughed James.

"Is it that bad?" Emma said looking squeamish.

James was about to have a joke with them but the look on his sister's faces made him change his mind.

"No. It was bad. But the last time the doctor checked it out it had healed quite good." he said.

James let the doctor look at the wound. The twins peered over his shoulder not sure, if what James had told them was true or if his leg was bad. They held their hands close to their eyes ready to cover them up if things got to gory.

"It looks great," the doctor told James.

"I think it would be alright for you to have a bath. Of you go Mary is in the bathroom running you as we speak."

James jumped up from the sofa and disappeared out of the door. Faster than a speeding train.

"Well that's strange. Mary was right. It's funny to see a lad of James's age so keen to get into a bath." the doctor remarked to Emma.

Emma laughed "James loves the water always has. He was trying to persuade mum and dad to get a swimming pool in the back garden. However, dad said there was plenty of water to swim in in the sea. However, that is too cold. I prefer the swimming pool at the leisure centre." Sarah piped in

"That's only because she fancies one of the life guards."

Emma blushed and said rather loudly

"DO NOT."

As she walked passed Sarah, she gave her a look of distaste.

"Think I'll go and see how the water baby is getting on" the doctor said as he made a sharp exit. The last thing that he wanted was to be involved in twin's arguments.As he closed the door he heard the two of them tease each other.

Chapter 39

The bathroom door was open and the doctor could see that James was enjoying the luxury of a bath. He decided to leave him and headed to the guest room. He opened the window and let the cool evening breeze wash over him he closed his eyes and he could hear the waves as they rolled to the shore. He thought about Andrea. He was sure that she was still alive but what he did not know where she was or if she knew about Julian. Although she was having an affair with him and he had been friendly with Julian. He never once wished anything like this to happen to them. He knew the situation. He had had an affair with Andrea but it only lasted few years. Things cooled down between them and Andrea and Julian tried to make a go of things. However, it never worked out worked out. The doctor went to work abroad to give them a chance. It was when they split for the second time that Andrea told Julian about James. Andrea told Julian that if he told James that he was not his father or he treated him any different from the rest she would leave him with nothing. For a while, he did as she asked but more recently, he had changed towards the boy. She did her best to keep James from finding out that Julian was not his father.

The doctor looked out across the bay and wished that he had persuaded her to leave all this and live with him at his father's mansion. He could start a clinic there. He would not have sold the one here. It was established and it was earning him a lot of money. He walked over to the bed. Kicked of his shoes and he lay down. Closed his eyes and drifted of to sleep.

James lay in the hot soapy water and thought about his time swimming under the sea. He followed shoals of fish. Swimming through seaweed letting it tickles him. He could see the jellyfish as the floated above him. There was no noise under the water. Everything was calm and silent. He listened to the noises of the house. In the distance, he heard the television. The twins were listening to some music. They will be dancing to all the music. They knew all the latest dance moves. He heard someone in the kitchen. Sounded like someone using the saucepans as a drum kit. Then he heard a strange noise. It was some one snoring. It came from the opposite end of the house. Then it clicked it would be the doctor he slept at that end. He lay still listening. He could not hear anything new but he had a strange feeling that there was someone watching him. He jumped up and turned round to see Jack standing in the doorway. James could feel his heard pounding. He wanted to scream but he was scared. His chest tightened. Surly Jack would not hurt him. Not tonight especially after, they had had a great evening. He even had him Conrad. He shivered even though the water was hot and the bathroom radiators were on. Jack closed the door and walked towards the bath. Jack saw the look of terror on James's face and said "it's alright I'm not going to hurt you promise. I just want to talk to you. If you want I'll open the door."

He turned and started to walk towards the door.

"It's alright. You can leave it shut" James said still unsure if it was the right decision.

Jack sat on the edge of the bath.

He cleared his throat and said, "I know that I hurt you really hurt you before but please believe me when I say that I am sorry. There is no excuse to hurt anyone the way that I hurt you. I would love to turn back the clock. I hope that you can forgive me. However, if you cannot then that is my loss because you are my brother and I would miss you? I want things to be the way they were or as near the way, there were. You know the way we used to fool around. Playing football, going for bike rides and walks through the woods looking for deer and at the wild life. Oh and most of all you will make the best uncle ever."

It took a few moments to sink in and James was about to ask what he meant when it clicked.

"You mean Beth's going to have a baby. You are going to be a dad. But you're not married."

James blushed as he realised that the last thing he said was something a child would say. He knew that you did not need to be married to have a baby.

"Not at the moment but if we decided to get married I want you to be the best man." replied Jack.

He did not pull James about not being married to have a baby, as he knew that James was a bit embarrassed. Jack put a hand up for James to high five it. Then as quick as a flash he grabbed Jack and pulled him into the bath beside him. The two of them splashed and carried on for a bit. The doctor heard the noise and went to see what was going on. He popped his head round the door and was pleased to see the brothers larking about.

"Watch your wound. In case you burst it open," he advised them.

"Yes we will" both the boys called.

Chapter 40

Mary was coming up the stairs to get the doctor. She was in a hurry and did not see him until they bumped in to each other on one of the turns in the staircase. She jumped with fright and gasped,

"Oh it's you. I was coming to get you there is two men waiting to see you. They are in the front room. I am just going to check on James. Then I will bring you in some coffee and tea."

She held on to the banister trying to get her breath back.

"You seem rather flustered are you okay?" he said

"Yes. Well I will be in a moment. I could not find you and I heard the door. I thought perhaps that you had gone out. So perhaps I am just panicking a bit. But I'll be fine." she said.

"I think you will be better staying away from the bathroom Jack and James are both in there having a ball. Jack still has all his clothes on. Do you recognise the men?" he enquired.

"No. but when they showed their badges I think it were from some international rescue group.," replied Mary.

The doctor's face whitened as he turned and took two steps at a time down the remainder of the stairs and went into the front room where the two men were. The two men were looking out of the window when the doctor burst through the door. They had been talking but stopped and turned round when they heard the door opening.

"You must be Doctor Newbury," said the taller of the two men.

He held out his hand to the doctor. The doctor came forward to greet the men. He looked closely at their faces to see if they would give anything away. Were they here because of Andrea? He thought. No what would she be doing abroad. She would never have left her children. His mind was working overtime trying to figure out why the men were here. As he approached, the man who was holding his hand out he suddenly thought of Stuart. He was helping to clear up after an earthquake. He shook the man's hand he introduced himself as Mr Bellingsire. He pointed towards the other man who was standing at his shoulder.

"This is Mr Jasper."

Who nodded? However, never spoke. Both Mr Bellingsire and Mr Jasper looked rather official. There suits were a dark grey colour. They had ties with a logo on them. The doctor recognised the logo. It was the same one that was on the letters that were sent to both him and Stuart when they both were enrolled in the company both Stuart an himself did a lot of voluntary aid work in there younger years. Stuart was part of their workforce. He had been on many courses with them and was now a training officer. Training the young ones who were coming into the company. Stuart often said that it was a great job and he loved the high adrenaline rush. Very different from their university years When Doctor Newbury thought his friend was going to spend his life womanizing and drinking. He pointed for the two men to sit at the dining table. Mr Jasper picked up a briefcase that was at his feet and the three of them pulled out chairs and made them selves comfortable around the table. Mr Bellingsire cleared his throat then said,

"We are here to inform you that Mr Stuart Greenlaw"

He hesitated as the door opened slowly. They all turned round to see who was coming into the room. When at first no one appeared, the doctor got up to close it again. As he approached the door, Mary's bottom appeared through the doorway. He hurried the last few paces to help her. He had forgotten that she was bringing tea and some of her home baking. He looked at a plate laden with scones and another with chocolate sponge cake. Looks tempting he thought. He might just be able to squeeze in a small slice of the cake. He took the tray from Mary and headed over to the table to the other men. The man in charge of the briefcase looked up from his rummaging through some paperwork. He pushed his case to one side and smiled in anticipation of the waiting goodies on the tray. The doctor notices that his buttons on his shirt were already straining and he thought it would be amusing if one of them popped open as he ate the cakes. He asked the two men what they wanted to drink and how they took it. Once they had their drinks and seated Mr Bellingsire continued.

"As I was saying we are here to inform you that Stuart Greenlaw has been involved in an accident whilst working for us."

"Is he alright? You would not have come here if it were a minor accident. How bad is he?" the doctor was now standing up.

He was clearly distressed at what he had just heard. He and Stuart had gone back many years. They had gone through college together. They were more like brothers than friends were.

"Stuart has damaged his legs. They have operated but he might lose them. He was working with some of the younger lads. They were nearly finished their shift when one of the lads slipped and came down heavy on a pile of rubble. Stuart went to help him but there was too much weight and the rubble gave way. Stuart was lucky"

"LUCKY" the doctor snapped, "how you can say that he was lucky he faces loosing his legs."

"The young lad never survived. We have just come from telling his parents. He was only seventeen" Mr Bellingsire cut in.

The doctor shook his head. There was total silence in the room. All that they could be hear was the heavy breathing from the doctor. Mr Bellingsire continued in a hushed voice

"The medics have operated on him but he has asked if he can be admitted to your clinic. He is waiting to be airlifted."

Doctor Newbury was pacing up and down the room. He stopped and turned to face the two men

"Please forgive me for the outburst. How are the young lad's parents? They must be devastated at loosing their boy.," he said in a shaky voice.

"There is one of out team with them. They will be there for anything they want. We will offer to pay for the lad's funeral. He, like Stuart was a great asset to our company. He had been with us for six month. He worked in the office but wanted to be out where the action was. This was his first time in the field. Stuart is devastated. He and the lad got on like father and son."

Not if you knew his real son, the doctor thought to himself.

"There will be no problem with bringing Stuart to the clinic. I will call and make sure that they keep one of the rooms free. How long do you think it will be till he gets here?" the doctor asked.

"If I can make a phone call from here to the head office they will get Stuart on our jet within the next few hours. When then the doctors give Stuart." Mr Bellingsire replied.

"Come with me" the doctor said

He led him to the hall to make that very important call. The doctor went back to the front room and waited with Mr Jasper. Neither of them spoke which suited the doctor. He wanted to be alone with his thought now.

Chapter 41

Andrea had managed to work her charm on the man who held her captive. She had lost track of what day or even month it was. She had managed to persuade him to let her walk about the house. Even though she had shackles on her ankles. He had also cuffed her wrists. This was terrible but it was slightly better than lying on a bed unable to move. At least she could go to the toilet. He even let her have a bath whenever she wanted.Of which she had taken advantage. It was a good way for Andrea to escape the situation that she was in She could almost loose her when the hot water eased her aching muscles. He left her on her own nearly every day. Sometimes he would be away for a couple of hours other times he was away all day and it was almost dark before he returned. She would sleep most of the time he was absent from the place other times she thought about her family which made her very upset. Deep down she knew that something terrible had happened to Julian but she did not know what.The man never said anything or spoke about him. She often thought about the doctor. How she had fallen for him when he was treating her after the loss of her first-born daughter Carla. She had kissed him in his surgery and asked to meet him the next day. However, when she got home and had time to think about the consequences and his reputation. How it would be publicised if it their affair had been made public. She decided that it would be best if she did not go ahead with seeing him. However, she had to go and meet him, but she would tell him that she just wanted to be friends and was sorry if she had stepped out of line. She fell in love with him even more as the years went by Things between her and Julian had ended. However, for the sake of Jack they still lived together. One night she had gone out for a few drinks with friends. They met up with the doctor and Stuart in a bar. Stuart just had back from doing charity work in Africa and the two of them were out having a few beers. The women asked if they would like to join them. Stuart she also had a thing for him. They all went to a restaurant and spent most of the night there. Andrea had managed to find a seat beside the doctor and the two of them flirted with each other. When it was time for them to head home, Stuart had asked if the doctor would mind if he were to escort the woman home. Deep down him was glad because that meant that he could have more time alone with Andrea. After Stuart had left, he took Andrea to a quiet little pub away from the hustle and bustle of the town. She remembered how they flirted more with each other. How they played footsie under the table. The softness she felt in his touch. The way his eyes smiled at her. She could see in her mind the way his shirt hugged him and showed of his firm torso.

Her hands glided over his chest as they danced to the slow music playing in the background. She loved the way he blew softly round her neck and ears. He would whisper her name softly in her ear as he nibbled her earlobe. She liked the way she felt when he held her tight. He made her feel special. No one not even Julian could do that. At the end of the evening, he had asked her if she wanted to come back to his place. She accepted without hesitation. Once they were there, his kisses were passionate. They had more passion than she had felt in her life He had turned her into putty in his hands and she liked it. He led her into his bedroom and there they spent the night together. Two people becoming one repeatedly. In the morning, they awoke to the sun shining and the birds singing. Together in one another's arms. For a moment, Andrea thought she had waked up in heaven. It was soon after that that Andrea found out that she was expecting. She knew that the unborn child belonged to the doctor. However, Julian had desperately wanted to make another go at there marriage. Confused she went to speak with the doctor. He had told her that he loved her, but he did not want to stand between her and her husband. He had told her that he would leave the area to give them a chance. She never told him that she was expecting his child. She let Julian believe that she was carrying his child. When the doctor returned a few months later, Andrea told him that the child she was carrying was his She still wanted to be with Julian and when the baby was born and looked nothing like the Costello's he fixed the results of a DNA test that Julian had asked for. There was a lot of stress going on in the Costello's life and their marriage broke up again. It was then that Julian found out that James was not his son. He was in fact the doctor, who by now had become one of there best friends. Julian had accepted this piece of information and he knew that Andrea held all the cards. He had become a gambler and had started to drink heavily all before he knew that James was not his own. She took over the coffee shops and kept an eye on the financial side of the business. He could leave but he would have nothing. Not wanting the humiliation, he stayed and let Andrea keep the business going.

A shout from the kitchen made Andrea jump. She had been lost in thought that she never heads anyone coming in. He shouted again. He burst through the door to the bedroom that Andrea had been held captive in.

"Seems like your boys a freak." He taunted her.

"Seems like he has got something wrong with him. He is weird. He hurt himself and I got some blood from tissues that he used to stop the bleeding. And guess what."

He paused as if waiting on Andrea to give him the answer that he wanted.

"He your lad James had some animal DNA in him. How's that then. He been crossed with a freak" he taunted her.

Andrea could feel the colour drain from her face. She knew what he was talking about the doctor had told her all about his dad and the experiment. He could not tell if the gene had passed to, James He had to tell her that there was no cure for it. Nor did he know what the future held for him or that of James. They had done tests on James every six months but they all came back normal. James never said he was feeling different. They hoped that he was clear. Now she knew what this person was saying. She had to think fast.

"What are you talking about" she asked trying to sound like she had no idea what he was saying.

"James. He was out in the moors and someone shot a deer. He ate some of the meat and he started running around just like a deer. He tried to jump a fence and cut his leg. I got some of these tissues and went tested them guess what?"

Again, he hesitated. Andrea just looked at him. She knew what was coming so she tried to think of some other reason of why there would be blood from the deer on tissues that James had used to stop his leg from bleeding.

"When I tested them there was deer DNA on the tissue he had been using. How do you suppose it got there?"

He was looking straight at Andrea.

She said, "Now if he had been touching the deer he would have blood on his hands he must have cleaned his hands with the tissue therefore there would be the blood from the deer on them"

She tried not to sound like she was insulting him. She did not know if he would get violent. He certainly looked like it at the minute. She watched as the look on his face changed. She could see him thinking about her explanation. However, would he buy it? She prayed he would. There were a few minutes of silence as he thought back to the moors. Perhaps she was right it might have been there because he had cleaned his hands. He turned and slammed the door shut. Andrea could hear him banging about and him curse. There was silence she thought that he had settled down and soon he would return and unlock the cuffs that she had round her wrists and remove the ties from her ankles.

Chapter 42

Graham stared into the flames of the fire. The whole of his plans had gone terribly wrong. By now, he should be sitting in some far of country with a load of cash that he should have got from Julian for the information about the DNA test that Doctor Newbury had rigged. However, now Julian laid a slab in the city mortuary. How was he to know that he was allergic to the chloroform? Then he decided to confront Andrea about her freaky son but he had that wrong to. Here alone in the kitchen he stared into the flamesof the fire and saw how things had gone terribly wrong. Everything had spiralled out off control. He knew that he had gone to far this time. He thought about the consequences of what he had done. He was already in trouble with the law over his so-called mother. The judge had told him that the case against his mother would stay on his record and if he ever got into serious trouble, they would consider it. The words went round and round in his head. Kidnap. Murder. Assault. Round and round they went sneering at him. Jail. Jail. Jail. He kept hearing repeatedly. He went to the cabinet where his father kept an array of whisky and other bottles. He opened a bottle. He did not look to see what it was. He just put it to his mouth and drank. The fiery liquid burned the back of his throat. He gasped for air as he coughed and spluttered. This was the first time he had ever drunk. He had seen the effects that it had on his mother and that of all the men that had accompanied her home. At a very early age, he decided that he would never in his life touch the stuff. Here he sat staring into the fire yet another thing he failed to do. All his life he tried to achieve things but it was the same every time failure after failure. He had finished the bottle. He felt sick. His head swam he could not walk straight he just bounced from wall to wall. He went to the kitchen and picked up his fathers gun.

He raised it to his mouth and said "This one I wont fail" he put the barrel into his mouth and pulled the trigger.

The sound woke Andrea. For a moment she was stunned unsure what was happening.She took a few seconds to get her brain into gear. Were there intruders in the place? Would they shoot her next? Were they her rescuers? Should she shout or should she keep quiet. She waited to hear if there were any noises. That might help her to decide if there was someone there. As it slowly kicked in she was alone and it looked like she too was abandoned that there was no one there she shouted for help where was that man. No, she thought he has gone and killed himself. In addition, he had left her here. Tied up like some pitiful animal. She felt Abandoned. She tried to free herself but the more she struggled the tighter the cuffs got. She screamed in the hope that some one might be close by. Silence surrounded her Nothing but emptiness. They, who ever they were had left her here to die through the night, she prayed that someone would save her. In the morning, she was still alone. Cold hungry and thirsty. She tried to move but her muscles were sore and stiff. She had lain on the bed tied up since yesterday afternoon. She called out for help but no one came. Her senses, like her body were numb. Why did her captor not come and release her from these handcuffs. She could not hear him walking around nor could she smell the wood smoke from the fire he lit every morning. As she slowly became more awake, she remembered. Last night. The way he came into the room and called her son a freak and how horrid he was. She also remembered the loud crack from a gun then silence. She turned her face to the window. There was no light. All the windows were covered. How she longed to feel the suns warmth on her face. She tried to imagine the wind blowing through her hair. Andrea felt her heart sink to an all time low. Andrea knew that she was alone waiting for a miracle. Perhaps death she closed her eyes and prayed for a miracle.

Chapter 43

Stuart Greenlaw was put on the jet an midnight and was due to arrive at the military base half an hours drive from the clinic in the early hours of the morning. The doctor informed the staff at the clinic that Mr Greenlaw was going to be arriving at the clinic. There was a room made available and everything was in place waiting for his arrived. The doctor had left the Costello's after explaining to them what had happened and promised that once he had made sure his friend was comfortable that he would be back. James watched him from his bedroom window. He was a bit upset because he was going to ask the doctor if he wanted to go fishing. He had cleaned all their fishing gear.

It was three o clocks in the morning. James had not slept. He had tossed and turned. He got up and opened his bedroom window. There was hardly any noise and he could hear the waves breaking gently on the shore. The light from the lighthouse flicked a beam of light through the darkness. Round and round warning ships of the dangerous rocks in the area. There were a few ships waiting in the water their light twinkling like stars in the sky. He looked up at the night sky there was no clouds. He could see the start of the dawn light peeping over the hills across the bay. He dressed quickly and as quietly as he could. He reckoned that he if he hurried he could get a few hours in on the water before it got light. He left the house by the back door. He knew that the police were waiting further up the road. He climbed the wall and went through the neighbour's garden. Climbed the wall at the bottom and went through the graveyard of the old church. He reckoned that if the police saw him they would not know who it was. He pulled his hood up and crossed the road that led down to the harbour. His dingy was where he left it last time he was out in it.

James jumped into his dingy and started the engine. He guided the dingy out of the harbour and headed along the side of the harbour wall. Once he headed to a spot where he knew it would be safe he dropped the small anchor and cast his fishing rod. All he had to do was waiting. He had not been out on the water for a while. He had missed it. He loved to fish. It calmed him. He sat waiting patiently hoping that the fish were hungry. He did not have long to wait. The line tightened and he saw the top of his rob bend. Excitement rushed through him. He gently reeled the fish in. He did not want to loose it. There might not be another. As the fish came out of the water, James could see that it was a big one. He took the hook from the mouth of the fish and as he held it in his hands, he knew this is what he had been waiting for. He decided that he was going to see what would happed if he ate all the fish. He bit into the scaly skin and he felt the change start almost immediately. He quickly ate as much of the fish as he could before he had to jump into the water. He managed to eat most of it. He jumped into the cold water and instantly he felt like this was his home. It was as if he belonged here. He swam down to the bottom of the seabed and looked around. At first, he did not see anything. He swam over to the rocks to see if there was any thing hiding there. Nothing. He swam round and round but it was as if everything had vanished. He was playing around by himself for a while when he noticed the little fish they were swimming in a tight ball.They were darting back and forth. He swam over towards them. He thought that they might dart off when he got too close. However, no he was swimming with them he could feel them as they brushed past his body. He could touch them and they did not bother. After a while, he went back to the rocks and when an eel popped his head out from between two rocks, he was the one who got a fright. He did not like the eel. The dull grey colour. The large mouth. Made him shiver. The eel did not seem to notice James. It eventually went back into its little hideout. He saw a flounder skim along the seabed. He thought that flounders were the funniest fish. They had a funny little mouth on the under side with the weirdest lips he had ever seen. He liked the way their whole body rippled as they swam. He thought it was as they were doing a Mexican wave all by themselves. He swam in front of it. Then he lay flat on the bottom and waited for the flounder to pass over him. He smiled as it skimmed over his body. It even kissed him with those weird little lips. This amused James He turned as he heard a clicking noise behind him. He knew what was making the noise but he could not see it. He turned round but nothing. He heard it again. He looked up and saw it. Above him swam the biggest dolphin he had ever seen. He hoped that it would come over to him. He knew that he would never be able to swim as fast as it would so he waited to see if it would approach him. At first, it looked like the dolphin was not going to come near him. He felt disappointed it was his dream to swim with dolphins. Looks like he would still have to dream. He watched it swim away from him. He waited until it was out of sight then he went back to looking around the rocks. He was looking at some crabs playing when he felt something nudge his legs. Startled he drew his legs up to his chest and spun round. He came face to face with a baby dolphin. He held out his hand and the dolphin rubbed his body along James's hand. James felt the smoothness of its skin. He swam after the dolphin. Together they played they swam round, over and under James. He played with the baby dolphin for what seemed a long time before it swam off into the distance. He wondered how long he had been under the water. It was certainly longer than any other time. He began to worry he headed to the surface. He broke the water's surface and was surprised to see the daylight. He had no idea what the time was but he figured out it was still quite early. He was about to pull himself back into the dingy when he started to have difficulty breathing. He tried to keep breathing but he could not and had to go under the water again. He started to panic. What would happen if he had to live under the water forever? He would never see Jack or the twins again. No one would know where he was. He would just have vanished. Just like his parents. He thought about how the twins had not coped after their parents' disappearance. How would they cope with loosing him? Suddenly he wished that he had not eating the whole fish. He thought that he would not like to live here forever it was fine form a short while but not forever. He swam back to the rocks and thought about what he was going to do. Five minutes or so had passed when he started to feel the change he was never so glad to feel the change. He was going to be all right he would see the family again and for once, this really pleased him. He kicked his legs as hard as he could, broke the surface, and cheered. He really thought that he was destined to live like a merman under the sea forever. He thought that the next time he would only take one bit of the fish. That is if there was a next time. He hauled himself into the dingy and pulled on his sweatshirt. He looked around to see if there was anyone out. There was no one the surface of the water was still. There was hardly a ripple. There was nothing to see either just ship further out still waiting on high tide so they could get on there way across the world delivering their goods. Alternatively, to pick up goods and bring them back here. He pulled in the small anchor that he dropped earlier to stop the dingy drifting. He started the engine and steered the dingy back towards the harbour.

There was a few of the old anglers sitting outside their little sheds on the harbour. He waved to them and they waved back.

He tied his dingy securely up as the side of a slightly larger boat. He clambered over it and climbed the rusty rungs of a ladder bolted onto the wall of the harbour. He went over to the men. He had not seen them for a few months. He missed their banter with him. They taught him almost every thing that he knew about the sea. They took him out on their bouts when he was too young to have his own boat. His mum would make up a picnic she would wave to him as they left the safety of the harbour. When they returned she would be waiting on the same spot, James wondered if she waited there all the time, they were fishing. He sat down on a lobster creel and one of the men handed him a cup of strong black tea. He listened to the men as they chatted back and forward with each other. Once he had finished his tea, he said his good-byes and headed home. The clock on the church was at seven thirty. He reckoned that he must have been in the water for about two hours. Possibly more he had no watch on therefore he did not know what the time was. He decided that he would just go up the drive to the house. As he passed the car with the two plain clothed police officers in it, he looked in the window. The same two followed them to the pizza parlour a few days ago. They were sound asleep in the car. James smiled as he banged on the window and they both jumped. Blinking they looked out of the window. They both looked puzzled. They had obviously forgotten where they were for a few seconds. James ran away before they realised what they were supposed to be doing. Not to fall sleeping on their job. James reached the bottom of the drive and looked over the house. It looked like everyone was still in his or her beds. Good no one will know that I have been away. He walked up the grass verge so he did not make a sound. He was almost halfway up the drive when a car turned into the drive. He thought it was the police men coming to arrest him he thought about hiding in the bushes but he knew that it was too late they would have already seen him. He kept walking not wanting to look back in case it was they because he would start laughing when he saw their faces. Because he would see their faces not how they were now but what they were like when he startled them from their sleep. He hurried trying to reach the house before the caught up with him. Which h knew was silly; after all, they were in a car he was on foot. The car drew along side of him and he saw that it was not the police but it was the doctor. He waved to him as he drove passed and parked his car beside James's new boat

. "Where have you been at this time of the morning?" he asked James.

"I couldn't sleep so I took the dingy out fishing," replied James

"Looks like you fell in your hairs still wet. Did you catch anything?" asked the doctor

"Yes but it was small so I put it back" lied James.

"You been out for long." he asked James.

Think it was after three when I left the house. By the time I got the dingy out could have been flourish. I met the old men when I came in. they were mending some nets. I think they are going out on one of the trawlers tonight." James chattered as they went to the back door and into the kitchen.

"How's your friend did he get back safely to the clinic. Is he going to be all right? He will not loose his legs. Will he?"

James looked at the doctor who was standing at the cooker heating up some milk to make James a hot chocolate before he told him to go back to bed and try to get some sleep.

James and the doctor sat at the table and sipped the hot chocolate.

"Yes he arrived safely. We have looked at his wounds and I think that he might not loose his legs, but it will be a long time before he will be fit and be able to walk. He was sleeping when I left but I am going back to see him later on this evening. Unless they need me before that. I need to get in touch with his son. Graham. He needs to know about his father" He said to James and thought to himself not that he would be bothered anyway.

"I will go to his work later on. Oh and I was wondering what plans you have for today?

He looked at James.

"Nothing just a bit of homework the twins brought me from school." replied James.

"Well how about. Once I have seen Graham and you have finished your homework. I have checked it to make sure it is right. We get that new boat of yours in the water." James jumped up from his seat and lunged himself at the doctor. Nearly knocking him of the seat he was sitting on. Hugging him in the tightest bear hug, he could manage.

"Great I'll do my home work right now."

James let go of the doctor and went to get his homework.

"No you need to get some sleep first. Do not want you falling asleep on the boat. I will get Mary to get you up about eleven. I should be back about twelve that will give you time to have a sleep and do your homework. Now let's get you tucked up".

They both left the kitchen and headed for the stairs. At the bottom, the doctor picked James up, threw him over his shoulder, and carried him to his bedroom. He dropped James on top of the bed and said, "You go to sleep and I will see you this afternoon"

James opened the window then climbed into his bed he drifted of as he listened to the waves roll to the shore.

The doctor went to his room and lay down on the bed. His head was swimming as he thought Stuart and the mess his legs had in. He was sure that he would not loose them but it was going to be a long struggle to get him walking again. He thought about Andrea and his heart crumbled. He thought that things were all going wrong. He prayed that Andrea was still alive and found soon. He buried his head into the pillow and cried himself to sleep.

Chapter 44

Nothing had changed since he had last been in the house. The hall was light and airy. The old oil painting still hung on the white washed walls. The chandelier twinkled with a rainbow of colours as the suns rays from the large windows on the roof filtered through. Pip his faithful dog bounded along the corridor to greet him. He ruffled his coat and then went to look for his father. He knew that his mother would not be home until nearly teatime. She helped run children's home on the main land.She always went to get the hair done and collected the weekly shopping and order things to be collected the following week. He went to the kitchen and made himself a sandwich. He shouted on his father but there was no reply. He thought that since it was such a nice day perhaps he had gone for a walk. He had noticed that his father had been looking strained over the last few months spending more and more time locked in the study sometimes he would be there all night. He had asked him if there was anything wrong. "No. everything is fine" he had always replied.

When he had asked his mother the same question, she just smiled and said "its nothing. Don't be worrying yourself."

She smiled and squeezed him tight. Normally he would have believed her but when he had looked into her eyes, he knew that she was not telling him the truth. He had gone out to the garden to see if his father was outside. The garden was in full bloom and the air was full of different smells from the flowers. There was no one in the garden. He looked out to the sea it was calm and there was no waves. It looked like a giant mirror he had to put his hand up to his eyes to shield them from the bright glare off the water. He might go for a swim later. First, he had to find his father and tell him about the results of his biology exam. He was the only one to get one hundred percent. Top marks. He has felt so proud and he hoped that his father would be equally as proud. He headed to the study. He should have went there first it has the most likely place he would have been he thought to himself. He knocked on the door and waited on his father to order whoever was on the other side to come in. When he was small, his father always kept the door locked and you had to wait until he opened the door. There was no answer. Strange he thought and was about to leave but he tried the door handle instead. Even stranger, because the door had always been kept locked.The door creaked open. The room was in darkness. He felt the side of the wall. Trying to find the light switch. His heart pounded. What if his father came in and caught him going into his study. He had never been in here for as long as he could remember.He saw afraid but also excited. His hand found the light switch. He hesitated deciding on wither to switch it on or to leave and just wait until his father appeared. He flicked the switch on. His eyes took a few seconds to adjust. He blinked. The room was quiet. There was a bookcase filled with book there was bottles of all shapes and sizes. He walked further into the room. He was going over to look at the books. Then he saw. There was a small walking cupboard. The door was slightly open. However, he still saw. He walked slowly backwards. He tried to get away from what he saw. His breathing came in gulps. His heartbeat was now racing. He felt sick. He started to shake. He thought that he was going to pass out. He reached the door and once there he had backed out, he ran outside the house screaming on the handy man to come and help. There was no one. The handy man had gone to collect his mother. He was left all alone with his father hanging from the light cable in the small walking cupboard in his study. He hid himself in the boatshed waiting on the return of his mother and the handy man. Rocking himself and crying uncontrollably.

The doctor woke up. He had not had that nightmare for a long time. He could not go back to sleep. He headed down the stairs and went to the kitchen. Mary was busy preparing some late breakfast.

"Oh it's you. I was not sure what time you wanted were getting up. Has your friend arrived safely?" she asked.

The doctor just nodded.

"Are you feeling alright you seemed a little pale?" Mary asked.

"I'll be alright things are just getting a little bit stressful at the moment. Nevertheless, I am sure once I see Stuart starting to get better and back to his old self I will feel much better thank you. I think that I will have a coffee then head over to see if his son is at work. I need to let him know that Stuart is at the clinic," the doctor said as he got up to make a coffee.

"I can rustle up some bacon and egg. It won't take long," Mary said as she lit the gas on the cooker,

"That sounds grand. Oh and if the smell does not wake up young James can you get him up about eleven. Make sure that he does his homework. I told him that we would get that new boat of his out on the water later this afternoon. Perhaps you can make us a little picnic. We might. If we are lucky bring home tea." he laughed with Mary.

He sat down and ate the bacon and eggs. He did not realise how hungry he was until he started to eat.

Chapter 45

The doctor turned his car into the car park of the City Forensic and Pathology lab he didn't see Graham's jeep but he went inside the building all the same. He remembered the last time he had been here. It was when he had to identify Julian's body. He asked the man on the front desk if Graham was in at work, as he needed to speak to him. The man wanted to know who he was and if he had any identification on him. The door behind the man on the desk opened and the detective who was dealing with Julian's case appeared. He came over to the desk when he saw the doctor standing there. The doctor asked him if he knew Graham Greenlaw as he was treating his father. As he was injured abroad and was flown, home last night and he wanted to let him know the situation. The detective told the doctor that he had not reported for work the last two days. They had sent a car round to the house this morning but there was no-one there. The detective also said that he had been acting very strange over the last few months. Very jumpy, always on edge. The doctor thought back to the time that he met with him on the golf course.

How he seemed nervous… He jotted down the phone number of the clinic and handed it to the detective

"If he shows up get him to ring this number."

He left the building and headed back to the clinic. He wanted to see Stuart.

When he arrived at the clinic, he spoke to the nurse who had been assigned to the care of Stuart. She told him that Stuart had had a comfortable night and he had managed to eat his breakfast. He went to the room that he was in. Stuart was sitting up in bed reading a newspaper. He smiled when he saw that it was his friend the doctor.

"You look a bit more colourful this morning. How are you?

"Oh! Glad to be back here with friendly faces. At least I understand what you doctors are saying. And if I must say the nurses are much prettier too." he laughed.

The doctor knew that things would always be the same with Stuart. Wine, women and song. The two men chatted for a while. The doctor was wondering how to tell Stuart that his son had not been seen for two or three days. When Stuart finally asked, "What has that Graham been up to? I phoned him a few weeks ago. He sounded agitated about something. I asked him but he would say."

Stuart asked his friend. "To be honest with you, I had a round of golf with him and he was very up tight then. Thinking back he got worse after I asked if it was all right if I could use the lodge," replied the doctor.

"Look you know that you don't need to ask to use the lodge. Now you've got me wondering what that little runt has been up to." Stuart said shifting nervously on the bed.

"I should never have let him know about that place. He would be thinking that it was his own. Would you do me a favour and see if you can get hold of him and ask what he has been up to. You have more right to be up there than he does,"

The doctor looked at his watch Then said, "I went this morning to his work to let him know that you are in the clinic. But they told me that he hadn't been there for a few days."

Uh! He will be up there pretending that he's lord of the manor. Not bothering to let anyone know where he is." Stuart did a little royal wave.

This made the doctor laugh.

"Listen do you want me to phone the police and see if there is anyway they could send a car up there to see if that's where he is."

"Christ no. he might think he was someone very important. I think that we should just let him sort himself out this time. I have had enough of running after his little arse. Should have let his go to jail and rot in there." he stopped for a breath and the doctor could tell that Stuart's blood presure was rising.

He put his hand on Stuarts shoulder and told him to calm down.

"You're going to make yourself worse. Let us just give him a day or two then I will head up to the lodge. Mind you if he sees me coming, he would be out the back door and off into the sunset. He knows that I will not put up with his rubbish. He knows that I saw through him from day one. Leave him to me I will sort him. I will not tell him that you are here. I will tell him that you want him to go away and stop bothering you. If that's what you want."

The doctor knew his friend and he knew that he would not be able to tell him to go. However, he could. He saw the change in Stuart. It was a worry. Stuart had aged so much. The doctor knew that because of Graham he spent most of his time abroad. "So" the doctor broke the silence

"What else have you been up to?"

There was a pause then a smile crept across Stuarts face.

"Gone and done it."

He looked at the doctor as if the doctor knew what he was talking about. The doctor frowned and said, "Done what"

Stuart took a large breath and said with a huge grin

"Gone and got me a wife."

He looked at the doctor who stood open mouthed. He then went closer to the bed and put his hand on Stuart's forehead.

"Are you hallucinating? Maybe you are worse than we thought. Can you repeat what you have just said?"

"I've got me a wife. Her name is Jasmine. She was has been working with us for about three years. We have to know each other better last year and we started to date six months ago. Then one day I asked her if I could make me a happy man and marry me. We tied the knot just before I left to go to the quake disaster. She came over last week to help us. She had to stay out there. However, I hope that they will get her back soon. You will like her. Sorry I did not let you know about her but at first, I thought that it would not last. After all you of all people know my track record."

He looked at the doctor as if he was waiting for reassurance from him.

"Can't wait to meet her she must be some lady if she has managed to tame you" the doctor joked with Stuart.

"Do you have a photograph of her?" He asked Stuart.

Stuart pointed to the wardrobe and said "in my bag. I you can bring the bag over herethen you can see my beautiful wife

The doctor found the photo and he had to admit that she was a very beautiful woman. "Where does she come from" he asked Stuart.

"She was bought up in Germany. Her family are in the forces but she has a UK passport."

The doctor looked at the photo again. She had short sandy brown hair and her skin has a summer glow. She looked gorgeous. He handed the photo back and then appologized

"I promised to meet James and take him out fishing."

"Have they found out any more about the Costello's? It must be hard on these kids and for you. Are you still living with the kids?"

Stuart could see that it was hard for the doctor. Thinking he should have perhaps kept quiet about Jasmine.

"On you go you can't keep the young lad waiting."

"He's only getting if he has completed his homework. He is still absent from school. However, he might be well enough to return to school next week"

He waved to Stuart and said, "I'll look in later. Who knows I might even have a nice bit of fresh fish for you. Just what the doctor ordered"

With that, he closed the door leaving Stuart to look forward to a tasty piece of fresh fish for his supper. As he walked away, he could hear the hearty chuckles from Stuart

When he arrived at the Costello's an excited James informed the doctor that he had done his homework. Who shouted at him as he was piling the fishing gear along side the boat? James waved excitedly at the doctor.

"I have got everything ready. My homework is finished. I got Mary to check it. Look she has made a picnic for us." James called to the doctor as he climbed out of the car.

The doctor went over to help put the gear in the boat.

"Have I got time for a coffee? And I need to check your homework" He said.

He saw the look on James's face.

"Promise it won't take long. I will drink and check at the same time."

James still looked like was desperate to go.

" tell you what you go and ask Mary to put the kettle on and I'll get the boat hitched up onto my car so that when I've finished the marking and the coffee we are ready to head down to the harbour."

This brought a smile to James's face and he scurried to tell Mary to put the kettle on. James went to the front room and watched the doctor reverse his car up to the boat. He did not have a name for it yet. You cannot put a boat into the water without a name one of the old anglers told him when he got his little dingy. They had sat on the harbour wall for long time thinking on a name. In the end, he decided on SEA PRINCESS A. The A was after his mum Andrea. The old men had helped him paint the name on the side. He chose the brightest blue he could find and hoped it was the same colour and the Indian Ocean. He looked at the big boat and wondered if you would be able to sail it to the Indain Ocean. One day he thought I am going to go there. He made a promise to himself. He went to the kitchen and waited as patiently as he could on the doctor finishing his coffee. Fifteen minutes later, they were heading to the harbour.

James got out of the car and waved to the old men. Who were still sitting in the same place as they were this morning?

"Look at my new boat" he shouted to them.

They got up and came over to give the boat their verdict.

"I she's a beauty. If you look after her she would last a long time." the one with the bushiest beard said.

"Is that why you're still here. The missus looked after you.," joked one of his mates

They all chuckled. James loved these men they were so kind to him. Helping him out when his rods had b been damaged. Showing him the ways of the sea. James thought of them as his grandfathers. He thought that he was lucky. Here he had four grandfathers when most people only had two. He never knew his real grandparents they had died when he was only a small baby.

"We are going out to sea with her would you gentlemen like to come along with us" The doctor asked.

To James's delight, they said that they would love to. Everyone played a part getting the boat into the water. Soon they were sailing out of the harbour.

"Have you thought of a name for her yet" the doctor asked James.

"Yes. I thought about calling her ANDREA. After my mum." He said.

He looked away from the doctor as tears stung his eyes.

The doctor put his arm around James and said, "I know it's hard for you at the moment. But things will ease."

James leaned into the doctor's body and slowly put his arm around his waist. One of the old anglers waved to the doctor.

"Here is a good spot," he shouted.

The doctor stopped the engine and everyone got their rods ready.

The man with the bushy beard shouted, "Let the young lad be the first to cast. He can make a wish and we hope that he has good luck with his new boat"

The rest of the company cheered as James cast his line over the side of the boat. Almost immediately his rod bent. There was a wave off excitement as he reeled in his line. He managed to land one of the biggest fish he had ever seen. The men all agreed.

"This boat is going to be very lucky for you my lad." Said the smallest of the old men.

"Now. Let's get some fishing done," said the doctor.

"I, just what the doctor ordered." shouted James.

Everyone laughed and they all got ready for an afternoons fishing. They decided that they had all had a good day and they should head for the harbour. Once they had secured the boat and unloaded all their rods and baskets. They shared their catch. Making sure that James got his big fish. They said their good-bys and the doctor took James home.

The kitchen was hustle. Mary was preparing the fish for their tea for tonight's tea. The twins were trying not to look at the fish as the doctor gutted and cleaned them. He asked Mary if she would prepare one for himto take into the clinic for Stuart. He would take it to him for his tea. While the fish was cooking, the doctor had decided that he would deal with the problem concerning Graham directly. He was going to find him and let him know about Stuart. Also, let him know that Stuart had had enough of his behaviour and that Stuart more of less wanted him to move on. He decided that he would not mention his wife.

Chapter 46

The doctor drove up to the lodge after he had eaten a feast of fresh fish and thick chips. The light was starting to fade. He wished that he had come up earlier. Whilst there had been a lot more daylight. He turned the car into the lane that led up to the lodge. The lodge was a good distance from the main road. He drove slowly up the lane, as there were many potholes. The lodge was in darkness and the doctor thought that he was not here. He drove the car round the side of the lodge. Graham's jeep was sitting abandoned in the small drive. He looked around but there was no sigh of him. He tried the door of the jeep. It was open. The keys were still in the ignition. The doctor shouted his name. All was still and quiet. He walked round the side to the back door. He fumbled in his pocket as he approached the door. He was looking for his keys. He could not find them. By now, he had reached the door. He tried the handle. It was unlocked. He opened the door and called his name. Still no answer. He swiched the light on. The small passageway between the front door and the kitchen lit up. He opened the door to the kitchen. It was in darkness. There was a strange smell. At first, he could not place it. However, as he switched the light on He recognised the smell. Rotten flesh. The smell filled his nostrils making him feel sick. There in a chair was the body of Graham. There was a swarm of flies buzzing round the kitchen. He sat in the chair. The shotgun was lying on the floor where it fell. Reaching into his pocket, he pulled out his handkerchief. Covering his nose and mouth, he wandered round the kitchen nothing else seamed out of place. He closed the door and headed back to his car.

Andrea had been alone for five days or was it over a week. She could not quite remember. She had been drifting in and out of contentiousness. She thought that she heard a car. On the other hand, it could have been the wind. She could not move. Not through fear but through stiffness. She drifted off again. The sound of a door banging woke her. Was this her captor coming to free her? She tried to shout but her throat was dry and her vioce was just a squeak. She prayed that whoever had come into the house would find her. No. The sound of a car driving off at high speed let her know that this person would not save her. She felt like weeping but she just drifted off into darkness.

Chapter 47

The doctor barged through the door of the pub and went straight to the phone. He dialled the emergency service and asked for the police. He gave the operator the information that they wanted and hung up. He went over to the bar and ordered a double whisky. The glass was no sooner on the counter when he lifted it and drank the contents in one swallow. He left the bar and stood outside waiting on the police. He waited about thirty minutes and there was still no sigh of them. He thought that he should have phoned the Costello's and let them know that he would be late. He was about to return to the bar when he saw the blue flashing lights. He waited until they had passed and then went back in to the pub. He needed another drink. This time he drank it slower. He was heading out the door when an ambulance passed him. They had their lights and siren on. He watched as it headed towards the lane that led to the lodge. He decided to follow the ambulance and when it turned into the lane, he thought to himself why had they called for an ambulance. Graham was certainly dead. As he turned into the lane, he two officers stopped at the bottom of the lane.

"I was the one who found the body. It is a friends place and he asked me to keep an eye on it. I need to speak to whoever is in charge up there."

The police officer looked at him and after a moment or two; he went to the panda car and radioed up to whoever was in charge. After a moment or two, he came back to where the doctor was waiting and let him head up the lane to the lodge. There was many people wandering about he manoeuvred his car passed the vans and the ambulance. He parked his car out of the way.He walked towards the lodge and a detective met him close to Grahams Jeep. The detective was dealing with the disappearance of the Costello's. He ushered the doctor towards one of the police cars. He opened the back door and told the doctor to sit in the back.

"What were you doing up here so late" the detective quizzed him.

"I was looking for Graham. In addition, as you said that you had been to his house and there had been no sigh of him, there I thought that he might be up here. This is his father's lodge. He had been working abroad. He has been airlifted home. He is in the clinic recovering from a severe injury. When we spoke earlier, he thought that he might be up here. I was going to come up tomorrow. However, I finished the things that I had to do and decided to come up tonight. It was quite a shock." replied the doctor.

"Did you look around the lodge?" the detective continued to question the doctor.

"No when I recovered from seeing Graham with half his head blown off. I thought that it might be better if I phoned you lot. Oh I think I looked around the kitchen to see if there was a robbery," replied the doctor.

Who was feeling that he was being treated as a suspect? He did not like this detective. He could not explain why. He made him nervous. Even though he had nothing to be nervous about. He turned round to see the ambulance men carrying someone out of the lodge and towards the ambulance. He could not make out whom the person was but he did see that the person was getting oxygen and there was an intravenous drip.

"Who is that?" he asked the detective.

"I can't say at the moment. However, she is in a very bad way. Starved and dehydrated. He had her handcuffed to the bed. Like an animal. Tell you something. If I found her and he was still alive I'd have killed him myself."

He looked straight at the doctor. The doctor shifted uneasily in the seat. Was he implying that I had killed him? On many occasions, I thought about it. However, never did. He thought to himself. He stared back at the detective.

"If you're implying that I killed him you're wrong. Why would I? Granted I did not like him but I would never kill him. Nor anyone else for that." the doctor replied angrily He was trying to control his temper. This detective is trying to blame him for the death of Graham and that of Julian he thought. Then in an instant, he thought that perhaps the deaths were related. Perhaps the person that was being lifted into the ambulance was Andrea. He frowned and ran his hands through his hair. If only he had checked the other rooms. He would have found her. That if it was her.

"Is that Andrea Costello" he asked the detective.

The detective looked at the doctor and he could see that he really did not know about her. Nor did he know that she was in one of the other room fighting to stay alive. The detective did not answer he just nodded. The doctor tried to get out of the car. He wanted to see her so badly. He had dreamed of this day. Ever since Andrea and Julian disappearance. The detective pushed him back down into the car.

"Just wait a moment sir," the detective said.

"I need to see her please," begged the doctor.

"Please" the tears stung his eyes

. The detective stood away from the car and lit the doctor go.

The ambulance men recognised the doctor and let him in beside Andrea.

"How is she doing?" he asked as he pushed passed them.

"It touches and go at the moment. We hade put her on a drip and she has been given oxygen" Replied one of the men.

The doctor looked at the heart monitor. The lines were squiggles of peaks and drops. At least there were beeps. As long as it keeps beeping, she will be fine. He kneeled down beside her.

"Andrea. It is me. You are safe now. No-ones going to hurt you any more." He whispered softly as he stroked her hair.

It had lost its shine. It looked so dull. The skin on her face was grey.

Her eyes were closed and there were dark circles round them. She had lost a lot of weight. She was like a skeleton with skin wrapped around it. He took her hand in his it was cold. He had never known Andrea to had cold hands before. They were always warm. He rubbed them gently.

"Andrea. I'm not going to leave you I'll be right here by your side."

He leaned over and kissed her forehead.

"I love you," he whispered and then he kisses her lips.

They were cold. He could not hold back the tears any more. He laid his head on her chest and sobbed uncontrollably. He kept hold of her hand. Gently rubbing her hand trying to get some heat into her. The ambulance driver wanted to know if she was stable enough to be transported to the city hospital. The doctor wanted to take her back to his clinic but he knew that the hospital had better resources. He told them that he would stay with Andrea. They wrapped her in more blankets. The doctor stared at the slow rise and fall of her chest. He felt so helpless. As they drove back down the lane to the main road. He kept whispering I love you. He was also begging her to hold on. Once they were on the main road, the ambulance sped up. The doctor took of the blankets and lay on the trolley beside her. He could feel her bones digging into his side. He put his arms around her and cradled head. He pulled the blankets over the two of them. He kissed her and whispered softly to her. Telling about the children and how much they missed her. How much he missed her. He told her that the new shop had opened and that it was doing well. He spoke of all the children and how they were doing. He kept watching the monitor. Praying that it kept bleeping. He told her that Jack had bought a boat for James. How they had gone fishing in it and how James had caught the biggest fish. He kissed her cold lips. His tears dripped from his face on to hers. He gently wiped them away. Afraid that he might rip her fragile skin. He stroked her hair remembering how it used to shine. He laid his head on her chest again and listened to the faint beat of her heart. Praying to let it get strong again.

The ambulance arrived at the hospital and the back doors flew open. The doctor was not expecting this and his heart missed a beat. The porters from the hospital helped get the doctor up from the trolley. Then pushed Andrea into the A&E. The receptionist asked the doctor a variety of questions. Was he the next of kin? Was he related to Mrs Costello? He answered them the best he could. He just wanted to be at Andrea's side. He looked at the clock. It was nearly nine. He was supposed to be with Stuart. He needed to let the kids know that mother had been found. Alive. Just. Nevertheless, she was fighting. He asked where the phone was. He phoned the clinic to see how Stuart was. He had asked the police not to let him know about Graham. He would. He wanted to go to the

Costello's house and tell them that their mother had been found. He wanted to stay here beside Andrea. He decided that he would phone for a taxi to pick up the kids and Mary. He phoned them to tell them that there was a taxi coming to pick them up and bring them to meet him. He asked the taxi company not to tell them that they were coming to the hospital. He asked a nurse how Mrs Costello was. She told him there was no change. He sighed and told her that if there were that he would be at the doors waiting on her children arriving. She was to come and get him immediately.

The taxi arrived and the doctor went to meet them as the got out of the car. He never spoke. He led them into a side room and once they were all seated, he said,

"Your mother has been found." he looked at their faces.

They did not know whether to laugh or cry.

"Can we see her?" Jack asked

"Yes but I need to tell you that she is very ill. When you go through to see her she will be hooked up to machines. But they are doing everything that they can."

He saw that the twins had huddled close to each other.

"It's alright don't be scared. Your mum needs you to be strong for her. Jack and James will be with you and I will be here with Mary if you need us.

"Can you both come in with us?" James asked in a small voice. "Because I'm scared," he said even quieter.

"Me too" replied Emma.

"Yes, we can all go together" Said the doctor as he opened the door and led them out into the corridor.

The doctor went to the receptionist and asked if the family could see Mrs Costello. She picked up a phone and dialled a number. She turned her back as she spoke to someone on the other end. She turned around and smiled.

"If you wait over there a doctor will be with you in a moment"

They all sat in the waiting room waiting. The hospital was quiet and all that James could hear was the ticking of a clock. He wanted to look at the time but he knew that it would not be any more than it was a few seconds ago. He tried to think what he could say to his mum. Would she be able to hear him? What if she was that bad and when he spoke to her she died. Jack and the twins would hate him forever. He started to get nervous and suddenly he did not want to be here. He started to rub his hands up and down his thighs. He started to breath heavy and he could feel the sweat appear on his forehead. His legs started to bounce up and down. He wanted to run out of the door. He stared at the floor hoping that it would open up and swallow him. He felt a hand on his shoulder. It was Jack.

"Easy tiger".

"Jack I'm scared. What if I talk to her and she dies. You and the twins will hate me." "She won't. She will want to hear from you so that she knows that you are safe and well. She will not die she has fought along time to stay alive she will not give up now. You know that she's strong."

He squeezed James in a bear hug

"You'll be fine we are all here for each other. You remember one for all and all for one. That's the Costello motto"

Everyone turned as the nurse cane over and asked if they were ready to see their mother. They all stood up and followed her along the corridor. The twins stuck close to Mary. Jack walked at the side of James and the doctor walked behind them all.

The nurse opened the door to a side room. There on the bed, lay Andrea the staff had cleaned her up and he was looking a bit better than she did when he first saw her. She still had then drip in her hand. However, they had taken her of the oxygen. She had slightly more colour to her face and her skin looked more white than grey. The doctor could see her chest move up and down more as her breathing had greatly improved. He saw the monitor lines were steadier. He knew that she was over the worst. He went forward and lifted her hand.

"Andrea you have visitors. Look the children are here. Mary. She has done a marvellous job looking after them. They have all come to see you"

He stroked her hand and hoped that she would open her eyes even if it were for a moment. He waved his other hand to urge the children forward. Jack was the first

"Mum waits till you see the new shop I've managed to get it up and running but you need to get there it still need that woman's touch."

He leaned forward and kissed the top of his mums head. Then he took her hand, lifted it up to his head, and held her hand while he made her ruffle the top of his head and said

"I've missed that"

Gently he laid her hand back down on the bed. He looked across to the twins and James. He smiled and mouthed come on its okay. Slowly the three of them walked towards the bed. The twins went to the side that Jack was standing at. James went to the other side. To stand close to the doctor. The twins were close to tears. Jack stood between them and put his arms around them.

"Look ma the twins are here and guess what. For once, they have nothing to say. You savour the moment cos we know that it won't last"

James slowly reached for Andrea's hand. Gently he lifted it to his chest and said, "Mum we missed you. But I want you to know that you were right here"

He pressed his hand as tight as he could to his chest.

"Every day we prayed for you. I miss you please come home soon."

The twins stood still. Not sure what to do. The doctor could feel there unease.

He said, " Your mum is just resting at the moment. However, she will be all right. You can speak to her if you want. She can still hear. Or if you just want to hold her hand that's just as good."

Sarah was the first to move. She placed her hand on top of Andrea's and stroked it gently she entwined her little fingers around Andrea's fingers. She looked at her mum and whispered,

"We all need you. We have one of you your gaurdian angle feathers. It is kept under our pillow. Every night Emm's and I talk to it and asked it to send our love to you."

The door opened and a nurse walked in carrying a bunch of flowers.

"This should brighten up the room a bit," she said

As she placed them on a table in the corner of the room.

"Who are they from?" asked James.

"They were in the ward they don't really belong to anyone. We just move them around.," said the nurse smiling at him.

Every one went over to look at the flowers.

Andrea opened her eyes. She tried to speak but she was too exhausted. She watched as the doctor, who had his arms around the twins, tells them what kind of flowers they were. She saw Jack standing with his hands in his pockets. She thought that he looked taller than she remembered. His hair was in need of a trim. He tried again to call his name. Her throat felt like she had been eating glass. She could not. It even hurt when she swallowed. She tried to lift her hand. However, she could only move it slightly. As she, lay there Andréa watched them through her half closed eyes She hoped that one of them would turn round.She tried to keep her eyes open but they grew heavier and heavier. Once more, she tried to move her hand. If only one of them would look at her. They would see her eyes were open. Even though they were slits surly, they would see. Suddenly they became a blur. Their voices faded. She tried to keep focused. Their vioces grew further and further away. Her eyelids took longer to open after she blinked.Then she plunged into darkness.

The machine screamed as the heartbeat from Andrea's heart was lost. The doctor turned. Shock and horror filled his head. He knew what that noise was. Flat line. No heartbeat. No pulse. He dashed over to Andrea's bed. The door was flung open. Two doctors dressed in white coats charged through the door and were at Andrea's bedside just in front of the Doctor Newbury. Mary stood clinging to the twins and James. She knew also, what the noise indicated. Jack slowly walked towards Doctor Newbury. The doctors were busy around Andrea. Eventually after what seemed a decade the machine started to beep. The two doctors turned around and one of them said,

"Panic over. It appears that the clip fell off your mum's finger. That is what all the noise was. We have checked her vital sighs and they are good. Perhaps she moved her hand and knocked the clip from her finger. However, honestly she is fine. Her heartbeat is slightly stronger. Which is a good thing?

Doctor Newbury went over to her bedside and took Andrea's hand. He smoothed her hair nwith the other and said,

"You gave us all a fright. Don't you be doing that again?"

The rest of the family came over and settled themselves down. The twins climbed on the bottom of the bed. Jack and James pulled chairs up and sat either side of the bed. Doctor Newbury said that he needed to make a phone call and would be back in about five minutes. He left them all sitting chatting quietly between themselves.

Doctor Newbury phoned the detective. He spoke to the receptionist. Who said that he was busy and did he want to leave a message. He gave her the phone number of the clinic and asked if he could phone him there. He hung up then phoned the clinic. He asked how Stuart was doing.

"He has been asking for you. I told him that you were on unexpected business and that you would come in and see him later.," said the sister who was on duty.

"I'm coming in shortly just got a few things to sort out here. I'll be about twenty minutes." Doctor Newbury replied.

He put the phone down and headed to the nurses station. He found the nurse who had brought the flowers in to the side room that Andrea was in.

"Excuse me. Can you please tell me how Mrs Costello is doing?"

He asked the nurse.

"Are you one of the families" she asked him not looking up from the computer that she was busy typing something into.

He hesitated for a moment. He was intrigued by the way, she was typing. She never looked at the keyboard and was typing very fast. When he used the computer, he had to keep his eyes on the keyboard and could only use one finger. He sometimes used to think that someone had shifted all the letters into different places. His thoughts were interrupted when the nurse asked again this time in a louder voice

"Are you one of the families?"

"Sorry. No but I am a very close friend. I have been helping look after the children." he replied.

She took her eyes of the computer screen and looked at him. "You look familiar." she said her eyebrows wrinkled. The doctor just smiled.

"What is your name?" asked the nurse.

"Newbury" he replied.

"If you wait a moment I'll get one of the doctors to come and speak to you. If you would like to take a seat."

He went and sat in one of the chairs that were against the wall. He could see the full length of the corridor. He watched the nurses and auxileries going about their business. They always smiled and said hello as they passed. There was not much difference between here and his clinic he thought. Not as many patients. The staff could spend more time with his patients. Here it was all go. A man popped his head round one of the doors and said that he could speak to him now. They shook hands. Doctor Newbury recognised him. He had come to the clinic for a job. Unfortunately, the clinic was not looking for anyone at that time. His

C.V. Looked first class. Unfortunately, the clinic could not afford to take on him at the time.

"How are you? I see that you managed to find work. Sorry that I could not take you on at the time. But I do still have your C.V. and I have kept you in mind in case anything comes up."

The doctor looked at Doctor Newbury with a puzzled expression on his face. Then the penny dropped.

"Ah you're the doctor from the clinic. I recognise you now. I got this placement here. However, I really would like to work in the private sector. I am looking but there seems to be a shortage of jobs. Now. Anyway about Mrs Costello. Her sighs are good and she has better colour. We are running tests at the moment to see if her liver and other organs have been damaged. She has regained consiousness briefly and we did manage to get her to sip water. We will continue with the drips for now. And she has had an antibiotis injection to help with the sores in her mouth and on her wrists." the young doctor said.

Doctor Newbury was happy with the information that he had been given.

"I need to be at the clinic soon. I will give you the phone number. If there is any change can, you please phone me immediately. The children and Mary will wait here until I come back. I should be about a hourish." he said

He scribbled the clinic's number down. Both men walked along the corridor towards Andrea's room.

It was a long drive to the clinic. What would he say to Stuart? How could he tell his best friend that his son had killed himself? He knew that Stuart did not get on with him but it was still his son. Stuart had been through enough at the moment. He had already lost the young lad who he had been working with. The one he had treated like a son. Now he had lost his biological son. He wondered how much his friend could take. He sat in the car park trying to get in his head what he was going to say to Stuart. He looked at his watch it was ten thirty. He felt drained. He had waited on Stuart arriving here this morning. It seemed like it was only a few hours ago. Yet so much had happened since then. He opened the car door and the cold air hit him like a punch to his chest. The clinic was lit up. He walked over to the door that opened to the reception area. The receptionist looked up and welcomed him.

"How is Stuart? He asked.

"He has been fine. He has a woman in with him. He seemed pleased to see her. I think her name was Jasmine".

This added further to his dilemma. Did she know about Graham? He would have to play it be ear. He asked if there was any whisky. The nurse looked at him.

"It isn't for me although I could use some. Earlier this evening I found Stuart's son dead. Unfortunately, I have to tell him. What's more, I do not know if Jasmine knows about him. Could you help me out.?" he asked the receptionist.

"Yes what do you want me to do?"

"Can you get the nurse who is on his case to go in and check his wounds? She has to tell Jasmine that she will have to leave the room. Can you take her a coffee while I go into the room and tell him the bad news? Oh and can you ask the nurse to take a glass of whisky in and leave it covered on the tray until I go in thanks. I'll be in my office let me know when Jasmine is out of the room and drinking her coffee."

He went to his office and waited.

The nurse was in with Stuart when Doctor Newbury entered the room as planned.

"Hey doc you just missed my wife. Don't worry she will be back as soon as they have finished with my dressings."

Stuart said when he saw his friend.

"Christ you look like you have been dragged through a bush backwards" he added.

Doctor Newbury waited until the nurse had finished and then sat down beside Stuart.

"Send in my lovely wife. The doc has to meet her." he asked the nurse.

Who looked at the doctor? He shook his head and said I need five minutes first… The nurse nodded and left the room.

"I went to the lodge. And I found Graham." the doctor said but was interrupted by Stuart who said, "Did you tell him to sling his hook."

The doctor stopped him

"He unfortunately has killed himself."

The doctor paused letting the information sink in. Stuart took a few minutes to realise what the doctor had just said . "Why? Do you know why?"

The doctor looked at Stuart. He was going to tell him everything he knew.

"I went to speak to him. His work had not seen him for a few days. I went to the lodge. His jeep was there. I went into the kitchen and there he was. The shot gun at his side. I went to the pub along the road and phoned the police."

He hesitated the next bit was going to be hard.

"I went back to the lodge. There was an ambulance. He had kidnapped Andrea. She was handcuffed to one of the beds. She was in a bad way."

Stuart stared at the wall in front of him.

"Did he have anything to do with the murder of Julian?" asked Stuart.

"I can't answer that. The police will want to do tests on the jeep. We will just have to wait and see. Does Jasmine know about Graham's existence? The doctor asked.

"Yes Jas knew all about him. I told her everything. Even about giving his mother the money to get an abortion. I thought that she would not want anything to do with me. However, she and I had a really god chat and. Well here we are. I think she wanted to meet him. Where is she I need to tell her?" Stuart said.

"I'll go and get her. But first I thought that you would want this." the doctor said as he handed Stuart the whisky.

"Thanks" said Stuart

He took the glass and swallowed the contents in one go. If you need anything, let me know. I need to head back to the hospital to get the kids. The twins will be exhausted. And James was up half the night fishing." the doctor said as he opened the door and left.

He got jasmine and introduced himself.

"Stuart has told me so much about you. I'm very pleased to meet you at last"

She shook the doctor's hand.

Then asked, "How is he. I have been so worried about him. He got so close to the young lad."

"I think that he will need someone like you around him for the next few weeks. Do you have somewhere to stay? I can ask one of the porters to put one of the guest beds in beside Stuart.

"That would be great thanks," she said sounding pleased.

"I'll sort than out. You can go back beside him. He's waiting for you."

He shook her hand again and headed off to find the porter.

When he opened the door to the side room, which Andrea was in, he saw the twins sleeping on the chairs their heads resting on the bed. Jack was standing holding Andrea's hand and talking softly to her. He looked up and said

"She has opened her eyes a few times. Briefly. However, she drifted off again. She knows that we are all here."

The doctor could see that Jack's eyes were red and he knew that he had been crying. "I'm so relieved. I thought that she might not ever open them again, and if she died she would never have known that we were here".

The doctor said, "I think she has passed the worst. She just needs to get her strength back. I will go and phone for a taxi. We need to get those kids to bed." the doctor said. He was about to head for the door when jack volunteered to go and phone.

"I need to get some air," Mary said.

Jack asked if James wanted to come with him and we can get a drink from the machine. James got up and headed out the door with Mary and Jack. He knew that the doctor would want to spend a little time alone with Andrea. The twins were sound asleep and they would stay that way. Once they were asleep, they were very difficult to waken.

Chapter 48

Everyone had just eaten their breakfast and was getting ready. The twins reluctantly were going to school. Jack had a meeting with the accountant. Mary was tidying up the kitchen. The doctor was going to the clinic and then he had to head into the city. He said that he would phone and find out how Andrea had been throughout the night. He came back a few minutes later and said that she had had a comfortable night and they could all go in later that evening to visit. He sat tat the table and made another coffee. The phone rang. Then Mary shouted for him. "It's the police they want to talk to you. Twenty minutes later the doctor came into the kitchen. He waited until James had left the room and said

"The forensics has done tests on the jeep. It appears they have found evidence that Julian had been in the boot of the jeep. Is seems that Graham had used chloroform to knock out Julian for some reason. However, unknown to Graham he was allergic to it and died as a result. They want me to collect things from his work. I will do that when I head into the city later. Anyhow, I had better head off got a busy day.

The clinic was quite busy. The staff had managed brilliantly in his absence. As he knew, they would. He had worked hard to start the clinic up. Now he was able to sit back and relax a bit. He called his called his financial advisor and made an appointment to see him. He wanted to check that everything was running smoothly. He went into his office and opened the filing cabinet. He asked not to be disturbed. At one o clock, he left the office and went to see Stuart. He chatted to him about what the police had told him this morning. He told him that he was making a good recovery. In addition, would soon be well enough to leave the clinic. They had long chats about their university years. Then the doctor told Stuart that he could go and have a holiday at his family estate. He would make sure that everything was arranged.

"Who knows I might even join you".

" well there's a first. I can remember a time when you said that you would never return there". Stuart teased the doctor.

" things change. I keep having the same dream. Remember the one that troubled me when I first started the university. I think I have to go back and face my demons".

" I'll talk to Jasmine and see what she says but I think she will agree" Stuart said.

"I'm going to collect the things from Graham's work. Then I have a few things to do. I will try to pop in later. Is Jasmine still here" he asked.

" no she popped out to the house to get a few things but she is coming back later"

Stuart said.

He sounded a lot cheerier. Knowing that he would soon be out of the clinic. To him being in here was like being a caged animal.

From his bedroom window, James watched the ANDREA bobbing gently in the harbour. He had enjoyed the trip that he and the doctor had gone yesterday. He could see the old men sitting outside their little sheds. Smoking their pipes. He wondered what he would be doing in school. His leg had almost healed. He was getting bored staying in the house. He wanted to go back to school. He would ask the doctor if it was all right for him to go back tomorrow. He went to his art box and started to make a get-well card for his mum. He drew flowers and hearts. That did not seem right. He took another piece of paper. He drew fish and dolphins swimming around a boy. A boy with fiery ginger hair. He drew jellyfish floating above them. Small shoals of fish that swam through seaweed. This looks better he thought to himself.

Doctor Newbury walked into the reception of city forensic and pathology. The man on the desk recognised him

"Come this way. Sir" he led him to the lift

. "They are waiting for you on the third floor"

He waited until the doctor was in the lift and went back to his desk. The lift door opened and a young man met him.

"Would you like to follow me"?

In addition, he led the doctor to a desk.

"This is the one Graham was working at. I am sorry for your loss. He seemed a sound person. Never thought that he would do something like that"

The young man seemed nervous. The doctor just nodded to him.

"Do you need a box or anything?

He asked the doctor

. "A box. Please."

The young man scurried of to find a box. The doctor opened a drawer of the desk. It was pens and note pads. There was not much in any neither of the drawers nor on his desk. No photos nothing that would be personal to him. He found a key in the last drawer. When the young man returned with a box, he asked if Graham had a locker.

"Yes it's over there".

He pointed to a few grey lockers in the corner. The doctor walked over. He opened the locker door. Deodorant a comb and a photo of James. He was in his little dingy he looked like he had been swimming. He turned the photo over. Written on the back was a date. Then twenty minutes this time. What did this mean? He rummaged through the locker but there was nothing else. He put the photo in his pocket and went back to the desk. He went through everything again this time more carefully. This time he noticed a piece of paper with the writing cross blood and a small scribbled picture of a deer. He looked at the paper then at the photo. The doctor's mind began to take in what was here. At first, he was confused he had done tests on James. They were all normal. Then he realised the by the time that James had reached the hospital his blood would be back to normal. Graham must have been close to James when he hurt his leg. Somehow he had managed to get some of the mixed blood from James Graham must have known about James but how. No one knew but Andrea and himself. It must have been when he was housing sitting. He must have found the letterform his father. The one he wrote before he hung himself. That was the only piece of information that was left. He had destroyed everything else. This was the last thing he wanted everyone knowing about him. This was why he did not want to get married and have his own children. He did not want them to be like him. When he found out that James was his he had to tell Andrea. Now James was like him. However, the tests had all been normal. He must have been following James. He had to have been close to him when he cut his leg. He would have got the blood before it had been through his body. He stared at the photo and felt like screaming. James would now know that he was not like any other boy. He would have to speak to him soon. H e piled everything into the box and left the building. He sat in his car and wondered what he could say to James. He went to the hospital to see how Andrea was.

The room had more flowers in it. Bunches all different sizes. Their scent filled the room. Andrea lay on the bed her colour was back. He went over to her. He lifted her hand. It was warm. Not cold as it was in the ambulance. He kissed the top of her head.

He heads a soft groan from her lip. He whispered her name. There was a slight flicker of her eyelids. He knew that she could hear him. He brushed her hair with his hand. He spoke softly to her willing her to come back to him.

Chapter 49

The sun shone through the window. James lay listening to the waves as they gently rolled to the shore. He looked at the clock on the bedside table. It was only five o'clock. He got out of bed and got dressed. He opened the door of his bedroom slowly. Just enough room for him to squeeze through. He knew that if he opened it too far it would creek. He tiptoed down the stairs towards the kitchen. The door was closed. He opened the door. He decided to have some breakfast. He went into the pantry and picked out what cereal he wanted. When he returned to the kitchen, he stopped dead in his track. There standing by the sink was the doctor.

"What are you doing up so early" he asked James.

Shocked and taken by surprise he was left speechless.

"It's a nice morning. How about we take that boat of yours out and do a spot of fishing."

James nodded. They headed down to the harbour in silence.

They climbed aboard the ANDREA and James stowed their fishing equipment. He then went to stand at the wheel beside the doctor.

"Are you going to the spot where we fished yesterday," he asked the doctor.

The doctor looked at James then said, "I know of a little spot further along the coast. We can try there. Here it is about time you learned to handle her. I'll show you what to do".

James took hold of the wheel and followed the instructions that the doctor gave. Soon the were at the spot. It was secluded. There was a small sandy beach surrounded by rocks. Seagulls cried and circled above. They dropped the anchor then set up their rods.

"It's just like a desert island here. I used to come here a lot when I was studying at the university. I could sit on the beach for hours and never see anyone. They cast their lines and waited to see if the fish were hungry. The doctor hoped they were. James prayed that they would not. The doctor soon felt his line tug.

"GOT ONE" he shouted to James.

James prayed that the line would snap. On the other hand, the fish would be too small and he would put it back. He looked at the rod.

"This was a whopper. It is putting up a fight. You always did catch big fish here" he called to James.

James frowned he was so hungry. He had up early this morning because he wanted to go fishing. He wanted to go by himself. The urge to be under the water was so strong. He liked the way that there was no stress or worry for him when he was swimming under the sea. He thought that now they had found his mother and she was going to be all right. The way Jack and he were now the best of friends. He would not have any more worries. The urge to be in the water would go away. However, some days. Like today, it was even stronger. This worried him. What was even more upsetting for him was that there was no one he could talk to. He felt so alone. He had a fantastic mum. Who would do anything for him? He was close to the twins and Jack. His best friend at school was always there to cheer him up. He had many people who loved him. He still felt alone. The tears stung his eyes. He tried to stop himself from crying. He thought about something funny. He tried to tell himself a joke. It was no good. The tears started to roll down his face. He turned his back on the doctor. He did not want to let him see that he was upset. The doctor had noticed him and knew that something was up. He had landed the fish and called to James but James never let on. He went over and put his arm around him. James pulled away.

"What's wrong?" he asked James.

James never answered. The doctor took hold of James's arm and led him below the deck.

"Think I need a coffee. Do you want one?

James nodded. He was sobbing uncontrollably. The doctor sat beside him.

"You can talk to me I'm a good listener. Is it your mum? She is going to be fine the hospital is happy with her progress."

He put his arm around James and pulled him close. He waited until James had calmed down.

"Everything has been tough for you this past few months understandably you will have found things a bit stressful. However, it is not god to keep things bottled up. If you want, you can talk to me and I will not be judgemental. Anything you tell me will go any further. And I don't think any-one out here will hear you it's only you, me and the sea." he waited.

"It's not mum. It is I. There is something wrong with me. However, I do not know what. I mean I am mot ill or at least I do not think I am ill. It first happened about the same time mum and dad disappeared. I was fishing. I got hungry. I did not want to go home. Therefore, I ate one of the raw fish. I started to choke. Alternatively, thought I was choking. I fell into the water." James stopped.

He did not want to say any more. The doctor decided not to push him into saying what was wrong. He knew what was wrong. He had been in the same position as James was. Fortunatly the doctor's father knew about him. He was there to help and talk to him. The doctor got up and made some coffee. When he had finished his he left James and went on deck. After a few minutes the doctor shouted on James

"Come quickly. Come and see this".

James climbed up the few steps and stood on the deck. The doctor was standing in just his jeans. James looked puzzled. The doctor picked up the fish and started to eat it. James could not move he be stuck to the spot.

"It's alright"

The doctor said. He threw the remainder of the fish to James.

"Come on join me," the doctor shouted as he dived over the side of the boat.

A few moments later James dived into the water.

The two of them swam down to the bottom of the seabed. They chased each other round the rocks. The followed a seal as it searched for food. The doctor picked up a handfull of sand and as he swan above James he let it fall back to rest on the seabed. James felt like a merman in a snow globe as the glittering sand particles sparkled on his skin. They found crabs climbing over the rocks. They watched the seaweed twisting and turning as the currents moved them along. A seagull broke the water and swooped down to catch a fish. Then swim back up to the surface and flew away to enjoy its prize. The two of them swam together side by side. It was so much better when there is two thought James. It was like a dream. Soon he thought I am going to wake up and it is all going to be a dream. All too soon, the doctor indicated that he was heading back up to the surface. James followed. The doctor treaded the water for a few seconds. Took a mouthful of air and joined his son in the water. When the effects started to wear off it was James's turn to indicate that he needed air. The two of them treaded the water. James laughed. Then the two of them got back on the boat.

The doctor looked at his son and knew that the time had come for explanations.

"James when I was a toddler. I went into my fathers study. He was working on an experiment. He was on the phone and had not seen me. I must have drunk some of the liquid thinking it was juice. He tried to reverse tests and find a cure. He never did. He gave up all hope and in the end, he killed himself. I have tried to find a cure but to no avail. I am sorry but now there is no cure. I do not think its life threatening. I have no other side effects and neither do you. You are healthy in every way. Julian and your mother spilt up for a while they were going to get divorced. I went out with your mum. A few times and that is when you came along. At first, I did not know that Andrea was carrying my child. It was shortly before you were born that she told me you were mine. Someone found out about my condition and me. He then found out that you were my son. He thought if he kidnapped your mum and Julian he would be able to extort money from your family. It all went horrible wrong. I do not think he meant to kill Julian or hurt your mum. However, you do not have to worry about him. He killed himself. I loved you, but I could only do it from a distance. Now I can be with you and Andrea. In addition, the twins and Jack. They have lost their dad. I will be there as a friend for them. I spoke to your mum this afternoon when I found out the story about her kidnap. She woke up for about five minutes. We had a good chat. When she gets stronger. We are going to have a holiday all of us. No one knows about us. You and me. It is up to you if you want to tell Emma, Sarah and Jack. Take time to think about it".

James looked at the doctor he tried to take in everything that he had said. He was saying that he was his dad. He had the same condition as him. In addition, most importantly he loved him. His dad loved him. He went over, flung his arms around the doctor's waist, and started to cry. This time they were tears of happiness. The doctor blinked hard he could feel the tears welling up in his eyes.

Chapter 50

Two months later Julian's funeral had taken place. The funeral was big most of the village turning out to pay their respects to him. Andrea had been out of the hospital and her strength was returning. The doctor had booked flight for them to go on their holiday. He had also employed the doctor that had been in charge of Andrea when she was in the hospital to oversee the running of the clinic whilst he was away. Andrea had helped organise the Beth and Jack's wedding. James was as excited as he was to be Jack's best man. He was busy trying to make a speech. The twins were helping with the flowers and the church decorations. Everyone had a part to play and there was a buzz of excitement in the air. The doctor had taken Jack into the front room and talked to him about his honeymoon. He handed flight tickets to Jack and said "you will be met at the airport and escorted to your destination" Oh and you will not need to pack many clothes the weather there at this time of the year is hot.

Andrea had met up with Stuart, the two of them had a long talk about what had happened, and she told him that she did not blame him for the behaviour of Graham. She hoped that he would still be a good friend of the family. Now the Doctor had asked her to marry him.

Two weeks after Jack and Beth is wedding everyone including Stuart and Jasmine headed for the airport. No one knew where he or she was going. The boarded a flight and settled in for a long flight to the America. Mary kept her eyes on the twins and James. Now that Mary had been asked to stay as the twin's nanny for the near future. When the plane had taken off and the flight was underway the doctor told them that they were going to Disneyland for a few days then they would meet up with the newly weds.

After the week in Florida the caught a private plane and the mystery continued.

"Do Jack and Beth know where we will be?"Sarah had asked

"Yes don't worry they are already at the final destination" the doctor teased.

Andrea was looking healthier every day. The sun had given her a light tan.She almost had her weight back to what it was before her ordeal.

"Can I sit up the front with the pilot" begged James.

"I'll ask the pilot but he wont tell you where we are heading" the doctor replied.

The plane taxied up the runway and soon they were on their way.

"Are you not going to tell us where we are going" Andrea asked the doctor.

He laughed, said, "And spoils the look on their faces. Look they have that look when you are opening your Christmas presents and you do not know what is inside the parcel. I am enjoying the suspense. Relax I know that everyone will love it".

He took hold of Andrea's hand and squeezed it gently. Looking out of the window he wondered if he would enjoy himself. He had not been back there for a long time. The flight was about four hours and the journey went smoothly. Once the plane had landed, they were ushered into a private room. There was food and drinks laid on.

"I feel like royalty. Did you arrange all this" Andrea asked the doctor.

"Yes. I did. Nothing but the best" he replied.

Are you going to tell us where we are going or at least give us a clue?" James asked. The doctor just smiled.

The airhostess came to take them to their next flight. They would be flying through the night.

"Hopefully the children will fall asleep quite quickly. It is a long flight but when you wake up, I know that you will love the place. The doctor said to Andrea.

"I think that I will fall asleep quicker I'm starting to feel tired" Andrea replied.

The children did fall asleep quite quickly as did the three women. Stuart and the doctor went to the small bar on the upper deck.

"How are you doing? I know that it must have been a hard decision to make. You haven't been backing home since your fathers death."

Stuart said to the doctor. The doctor took a mouthful of lager and then said

"I had no intention of returning to the family home. After the death of my father, it was hard for my mother and she died of a broken heart six months later. I turned the house into a hotel. Everything was running smooth. Never the less I could not stay there. There were too many bad memories. I had to leave. I never intended on getting married nor having any children. However, things have changed I have James to think of now. It's only right that he should see where his ancestors came from."

He took another mouthful of the cool lager.

"Well doc I'm looking forward to see where my best mate comes from. Does Andrea know about your accident"? Stuart asked the doctor.

"Yes unfortunately James had taken the gene on as well. The poor lad was quite confused. I think he understands things better now. After I had a chat with him," the doctor replied.

Stuart knew about the doctor. Stuart was there for him when things got hard and he needed someone to be there for him. The two of them finished their pints in silence then headed back to catch some sleep themselves.

The plane landed early in the morning. It was already getting hot. They came off the plane. Soon they were ushered onto another private plane and soon they were taxing up the runway again.

"This is like a magical mystery tour". Emma squeaked.

They were soon up in the air. James looked out of the small window at the city slowly get smaller and smaller.

"Look James down there. That is the Indian Ocean. See how blue the water is. Just like your eyes" his mother said pointing at the vast blue sea below them.

"See that island over there," the doctor said

"That's where we are going"

The plane circled a large three-story house. Two people were waving on the lawn.

"Look" cried Sarah

"It's Jack and Beth"

The pilot announced that they would be landing and could everyone take a seat and fasten their seatbelts. The doctor sat with James and said

"Wait till we swim in waters around here. It's a different kettle of fish," James giggled at the last thing his dad had said

"Is there sharks in the water" asked James

"Just friendly ones. There are many colourful fish. The best thing about the water here is that it is warm.

The doctor looked at the passengers and every one of them looked different. Like a huge weight had been lifted of their shoulders. He looked at James. He hoped that he now would be able to be a father to him. Not stand and watch from the sidelines.

Lightning Source UK Ltd.
Milton Keynes UK
UKOW02f2043191216
290410UK00001B/1/P